Beauty Sleep

Books in The Looking Glass Saga:

LOOKING GLASS SAGA

BOOK SIX

TANYA LISLE

SCRAP PAPER ENTERTAINMENT

Scrap Paper Entertainment
www.scrappaperentertainment.com

Contents

CHAPTER 1

One Last Christmas

DIVORCE HAD BECOME a forbidden word. It hadn't even appeared in the emails telling Alice that she was going directly to the Case's for Christmas break and that she would be remaining there until the school year started. Now that she was here, it was a topic that would not be brought up, though it seemed that there were more than a few close calls in the first couple days.

Alice wondered if that was for her benefit or if she was going to have to tell them that not talking about it wasn't going to stop it from happening.

It was a little sad, but she could understand why they didn't want her there right now. She hoped that she could see her parents one last time before she was taken away forever. They wouldn't miss her, though. She wasn't sure they would miss her even if they did remember that they had a daughter. She had caused them a lot of problems, had likely been the cause of their divorce despite what Lori tried to tell her. Maybe with her gone they could work out their problems and be happy. Just one more semester.

She could send them an email or call them before the Bandersnatch took her away. Evan's disappearance had taught her that the Bandersnatch didn't seem to be as good at cleaning up electronic evidence. Not that either of them would know what her email was about after June.

Again, she found herself wondering if there was really a point to trying to say goodbye to anyone before she was taken away. The point was to give them some closure about her disappearance and to let them know she was thinking of them and sorry, but it meant nothing once she wasn't there anymore. When he took her, it would be like she never existed.

Statistically, there was a chance she might be able to figure out a way to get around the Bandersnatch. There was likely *some* way to convince him to leave and to win the bet, but all of her looking through the books and trying to work out a method of trapping him or throwing him back into Wonderland had so far proven fruitless. She didn't have any more ideas.

There was nothing to do but try to finish as much as she could before she was gone once and for all. Hopefully Adam would come back without too much of a fight, and she could find Matt before it was all over. She should do something about the Queen of Hearts, but Wonderland could probably figure that out without her. She would need to teach someone else to return hearts, but that was it. If she could just finish that, maybe she could find some time to have a bit of fun before she faded away.

For right now, though, she tried not to think about it, even though it continued to creep into her thoughts at every waking moment now that she was enjoying her very last Christmas. Adrianna was off with one of her brothers doing something else, leaving Alice and Lori to hang out with Ryan and Travis as they prepared cookies for tomorrow. Again.

Cookies had become a thing Alice was making more or less constantly while she was here, seeing as they were eaten with fair regularity. While the people in the Case household were mostly their usual selves, kind and friendly, there were still flashes of hostility that came out of nowhere. Peter had shown her which flower would dispel that and so she had made it a point to be in the kitchen at least a little each day to sprinkle a some of the cure in the food so that she would not have to deal with that any longer. She wasn't sure how much longer the flowers would last, but she had far too much on her mind to be worried about that as well.

"My baby sister's almost in high school!" Lori said, pleased as they put the cut cookies in the oven and set the timer. Alice was careful to be the one to make the dough, remembering all too well how Lori tended to forget ingredients like sugar when she was baking. "New classes, new dorms, new everything."

"Except Addie," Travis told her. "You don't get to lose her just yet."

Alice smiled, though she felt a pang of guilt at the reminder. She was going to be abandoning Adrianna to high school all on her own. She would be all right, going in with plenty of friends who could give her a hand and without Alice to distract her from her classes any longer, but perhaps she was someone she should say farewell to before she left. Or maybe not. If she was gone the next day, it would be easier for everyone and they wouldn't have to be sad at all.

"I have to get there, first," Alice reminded her, a smile on her face. It was out of her hands now, and there was no reason to make anyone else worry about it. She would be gone no matter what happened. And it was Christmas in a house that really liked celebrating the holiday with family. Who had basically been adopting her the last few years. And with a sister that she thought she might never see again. She could let herself relax at least a little.

"You'll get there," Lori said, ruffling her hair a little. "Ms.

Miller taught you all this stuff years ago. You could probably have jumped right into high school with her help if you really wanted to."

"Does that mean she can tutor you in Chemistry?" Ryan asked, looking over at the pair of them. "Because I saw that last test." He smiled gently, though Lori looked embarrassed about her grades and stumbled through an explanation.

"Not my fault that teacher *hates* me," she said. "I missed *one* question on the test and the whole multiple choice was off after that." She looked and sounded irritated from the whole thing, but Alice still smiled and tried to gently calm her back down. She didn't want Lori to be upset during their last Christmas together.

"Can you retake it?" Alice offered.

"Yeah, I'm doing a makeup exam with a different teacher in January," Lori told her. "No scantron, so I shouldn't screw it up this time around." That seemed to calm her down, or at least she pushed the feelings back down before they could boil over. Alice could tell she had already been stressed about this enough, so she didn't press any further. Ryan looked like he wasn't sure if he'd said something wrong, but neither of the girls would say anything.

"Is your girlfriend coming tomorrow?" Alice asked, trying to divert the subject to something a little happier. She did like seeing her sister happy, and knowing that she was in a relationship and watching her light up talking about it was one of the things Alice had come to enjoy. It was great spending so much time with Lori this year, but she did hope that she wasn't taking her away from other people in her life. Well, maybe she was okay with it since it would only be one last time. "Her name is Jennifer, right?"

"She's coming by for lunch on Boxing Day," Lori said, already looking excited. "But I'm going to be heading there for dinner tonight. You're okay with putting up with all these guys without me for a night, right?" She smiled, looking up directly at Travis, who looked offended.

"Hey!" he snapped back at her, but he was smiling as he said it. "What's that supposed to mean?"

"I think you know exactly what it means," she told him.

"I think you need to elaborate."

"I think *you* need to learn how to peel a carrot again."

Travis jumped and realized that he wasn't so much peeling the carrot anymore as he was whittling it into a very sharp point. Ryan laughed as Travis put it casually to the side, patting it like it could keep his secret, and moved onto the next one. "You know, if someone tried to attack us right now, I could protect us all with Frosty's nose. You should be thanking me."

"Thank you for turning a nose into a murder weapon," Ryan told him, giving him a light whack on the back. "Now, if you could continue cooking like there were still two extra ravenous mouths to feed, that would be great." Even as he said it, confusion flickered across Ryan's face like he wasn't sure what he was supposed to make of it. He shook the thoughts away. Alice looked back at the timer for the cookies.

She had to get Adam back, at least. Before she was gone forever, she needed to find a way to make him come back. He knew she only had a little time left, but she didn't know for sure if he was actually going to do what he said and actually come back of his own accord. Maybe Tiger Lily could try and force him back across. Or maybe Peter could go and get him back. If he remembered her well enough to do this one last thing for her.

"What do you think's going to happen next year?" Alice asked Lori, letting the brothers have their shenanigans while she talked to her sister. She wasn't going to be around, but she did want to make sure Lori was going to be all right with all the changes happening with their parents. She had said things in the past that made her wonder. "When they're divorced, will you still live here?"

"If they'll let me," Lori said with very little hesitation, though her voice was low as room went very quiet. No one had said the word yet, and it was apparent from the way Ryan and Travis were looking at her that it had been for Alice's sake. "Unless you really want me to be there. When you're living with mom, maybe she'll let me come back if you really need me."

"They'll let you stay," Alice told her, smiling. If Lori didn't want to move, then she wasn't about to make her. There was no reason to force her to move if Alice was not even going to be in the picture for much longer. Instead, she could be comforted in knowing that she was going to be alright in the end. She could live on happily with her girlfriend and friends, and with the Cases around if anything did go wrong.

Lori smiled at her and gave her a hug. "I'm sure they will," she said. "Mom might move out here. I don't know if you've talked to her much. She told me once she had someone offer her a job in New York. She might transfer out here if you want to hang out more often, just the two of us without all these guys."

"Hey!"

"Excuse me," Lori said to Travis, laughing as she tried to look offended. "Can't you see that I'm talking to my sister?"

"You think she'll really come out here?" Alice asked. Part of her wondered if they would actually still get divorced if Alice wasn't a factor in their lives anymore. Despite what Lori said about this being more about her, Alice wasn't sure how she could have anything to do with it if she hadn't even been there for years. But if they were still apart, it would make sense for her mother to get far away from the man she had once fallen for. "I guess they won't be living together when it's done."

"That's not really how a divorce works," Lori told her, giving her shoulders another squeeze. "At least you aren't stuck there listening to the fighting. But if you need anything at all, you know where I am. Right here. Failing Chemistry. Or at Jenn's house, also failing Chemistry, no matter how hard she tries to help."

"Might help if you guys actually studied," Ryan suggested from across the room.

Lori grabbed a spatula and chucked it across the room, Ryan plucked it out of the air before it hit him and laughed. The tension seemed to have fallen away and they finished making cookies. Lori packed away some to bring with her to Jennifer's house and left Alice, promising that she would see her in the morning and that they would talk more if Alice needed it. Alice smiled and let her go, not sure what she was so concerned about.

Granted, she thought Alice was going to go back one day.

Dinner, even without Lori, was as fantastic as it ever was, and Midnight Mass was just as strange as it had been before. Alice still didn't really understand what was going on. It was a tradition for the Cases, though, and they seemed comfortable with the motions. Again, Alice just tried to follow along with the movements and tried to be polite about the whole matter, but stayed sitting with Ryan when the rest of them went up to take communion.

Alice was exhausted by the time they got home and headed back to her room, hoping to fall asleep and not think too much about anything until Christmas in the morning. The hand that grabbed her by the arm as she reached her room had other ideas.

She turned to see Lance there, standing by Adrianna with a serious look on his face. He had been trying to corner her since she had gotten there. Alice had done her best to avoid him, to keep from having to listen to him apologize again for trying to kill her last semester. She was too tired to protest now and could only hope he would make it quick.

"Yes?" she asked. She blinked at him, and looked to Adrianna. Strange that she looked concerned as well. Adrianna had accepted that Alice forgave her and hadn't tried to apologize again, so there was no reason for it. She tried to think of what else might have caused that look, something that would mirror whatever Lance was looking to say. "I haven't been looking for Matt," she told them, taking a guess at what it was. "I haven't gone over at all since last time."

"That's not what we want to ask about," Lance said. "We know you haven't been over there. When would you have time? We want to know about the Bandersnatch thing. You've been kind of on edge. We wanted to make sure you had this whole thing under control and you had it figured it out. If you need a hand with it, you know we'll do what we can to help you out."

Alice's eyes darted down the hall, checking for anyone who might be listening as her mind raced. It figured they would ask. She had to tell Adam the truth, if only so that he might listen to her and actually leave when she needed him to. But for everyone else, they didn't need to know. Not if she was going to be allowed to finish everything without being interrupted.

"We don't want you to disappear," Adrianna added.

Alice resisted the urge to remind her that she wouldn't even know that Alice was gone when she was taken. It would be like she never existed. New memories would replace her and make it a seamless transition. She would never have been part of their lives. She had seen it with Sarah and Evan already, and knew just how easy it would be for everyone to move on. There was no reason to worry them.

Alice smiled comfortingly and shrugged. "I dealt with it before I left," she told them. "The Bandersnatch is already gone. I thought I mentioned it. Sorry."

"That's great!" Adrianna said. She was genuinely happy for her, looking like she was about to catch her up in a hug to celebrate, but Lance stayed in the way. He kept holding Alice's arm, not squeezing any tighter, just keeping her there while he watched her carefully. Alice kept eye contact with him. Eye contact was generally what made people believe her.

"What do you mean you dealt with it?" Lance pressed. "That seems like the sort of thing you should mention before now. Maybe like you should have mentioned it as soon as you did it. When?" His eyes lingered back to the healing bruises on her neck. He looked away, a flush of shame crawling onto his face.

Alice shrugged. "There was a page in the red book," she said. "But I won the bet, so it's over now. No more disappearing." She smiled and tried to look relieved about the whole thing. It looked like it might be enough to make Lance to let her go. At first.

He narrowed his eyes on her and tried to figure out what in this whole equation seemed funny. He knew something was off, but he couldn't quite place what it was. "Then why have you seemed kinda... off since you got here?" he asked. "You're usually different."

This one was an easy one. "My parents are getting divorced."

Lance seemed to be suddenly aware of the hand he had on her arm and plucked it away. He grabbed his own elbow, looking embarrassed about his actions but unwilling to say so. "Well, you don't have to deal with that right now," he said, avoiding her eyes. He started to turn, his body desperate to take him far away from there. "I'll see you in the morning."

As soon as he moved out of the way, Adrianna caught her in a hug. "I'm happy you're not going to disappear!" she told her, hugging her tight. "And I'm sorry your home's not going to be good when you get back to it. But you can always come here if you need to."

Alice smiled, though her heart dropped. "Thanks," she said. "We should get to sleep. It's Christmas in the morning!" With that, Alice headed back into her room so the exhaustion could finally take over.

CHAPTER 2

Future Plans

CHRISTMAS HAPPENED WITH all the chaos and laughter that Alice had grown accustomed to. No matter how much Alice might have wanted to spend time with her parents, she knew she was much happier spending the day with the Cases. Even Claudia was pleasant, joking and laughing with the rest of the family and talking to Alice like she didn't try to have her killed last semester. Alice didn't want to ruin the day by bringing that up and went with it, though was sure to make sure everyone had plenty of cookies.

The only remarkable thing that happened was a gift from her mother. Alice hadn't been expecting anything from her parents, assuming they were both far too busy with the divorce to remember her, but a small package arrived for her wrapped in gold. Inside was a phone and a letter from her mother reminding her that she could call whenever she wanted. Alice was sure to call her on it to thank her before it was passed around and properly set up by the Cases, who were much more interested in it than she was.

Lori's girlfriend joined them for lunch the next day. Jennifer stayed quiet no matter how Travis tried to get her to open up, and she spent the meal clinging to Lori's hand. Even Mr. Case tried, but Jennifer only grew more quiet and shrank behind Lori the more people looked at her. Alice knew the feeling and didn't try to push, instead paying attention to how happy Lori was.

In the end, Alice didn't need to talk to her. Jennifer looked like she was making Lori happy and that was all she really wanted to know. After everything, Lori should be happy. And she should probably pass Chemistry, but Ryan was annoying her enough about that.

Jennifer lingered into the afternoon until she had to head back home to her family. As she left, she stopped Alice for only a moment. "It was nice meeting you," Jennifer said quietly. She smiled warmly and met Alice's eyes for only a moment before turning back to the Lori.

"I'll walk you home?" Lori offered.

Jennifer said something to Lori, voice so low that Alice couldn't make it out, but she left alone.

Lori was glowing and smiling a carefree smile that Alice didn't think she had ever seen on her. "She's not good with a lot of people," she explained. "Maybe we can do something with just the three of us over spring break this year. You should come here."

That was not happening. Alice needed to do too much in Wonderland that she would never have enough time to come back. And, even if she did, it was going to be hard enough saying goodbye this time. She wasn't going to make herself do it again. "Maybe," Alice said, smiling.

She was almost certain Lori could see through the plastic smile on her face, but she did it anyway. There was something in the way Lori looked at her that told her she did not believe her. Alice nodded and kept looking her in the eyes. "I'm going to see if Ryan needs any help," she said.

Lori let her go, but Alice could see the start of a frown on her face as she turned away. "Tell him we can just have left-overs," Lori called after her, loudly enough that Ryan could probably hear her. "He doesn't need to cook again!"

Claudia was a very unexpected presence in the kitchen, largely because Ryan had more or less banned her from there in order to keep things from being burnt. Alice's pace slowed as soon as she saw her, not sure if the Christmas truce was over or if it had ever been real in the first place.

"Don't you have a New Year's gala to plan?" Ryan asked, failing to be nice about her presence. "Or literally anywhere else you could be? You just *being* in here is making me think something is going to catch fire. Or spoil. Or spoil then spontaneously combust."

Claudia laughed, but she didn't move from her seat at the breakfast bar. "Maybe I'm trying to convince everyone to go out for dinner today," she suggested. "If there's nothing to eat..."

"Devious," Ryan told her, continuing to attempt to make pasta for the house. "Hey," he called to Alice when he noticed her standing there.

"Hey. Did you need a hand?"

"Can you tell your sister that there's no leftovers left after lunch? We *need* to cook."

"Or," Claudia said, leaning across the counter. "Pizza."

She looked normal enough, but just a little too much like she could have been Adrianna's mother for comfort. She was also the source of too many issues that Alice had had over the past year. She didn't know what to say to someone who was sending her adopted children after her just to try and get a book.

It wasn't entirely unprovoked, she had to admit at least that much. Alice had stolen it.

"Ryan, could you give us a minute?" Claudia asked. She sounded pleasant enough in her request, but Ryan left in that fashion that was so automatic that Alice knew he was bewitched. He didn't even turn off the heat on the stove, the meat sauce continuing to cook while he walked away.

Alice jumped into the kitchen, taking over dinner and Claudia leaning over the counter to watch her cook in his place. Alice wasn't going to be intimidated by her and took this as her chance, grabbing the small vial of flower petals and scattering a few of them over the sauce, giving it a stir and hoping that no one would notice that the sauce tasted a little floral this time around.

"Another little witch," Claudia said, looking her over carefully as she kept cooking. "It would figure."

Alice said nothing. She wasn't a witch, not green or imbued with magic or anything like that. She had learned words and actions that did strange things, maybe, but she had also fallen victim to pastry enough times that she was sure that disqualified her from ever being considered any sort of credible magician. Witch was giving her far too much credit.

"I want my book back," Claudia told her after the lack of response. "I know you took it, even if I haven't been able to find it yet."

Alice wondered if there was a point in confessing. It was obvious that Claudia knew she took it and was still trying to use her family to get it back. There was no point in hiding it now. She was going to be gone soon enough. And when she was gone, Claudia could continue without her, chasing after whatever Alice had done with the books.

Alice would have to figure out what she was going to do with the books when she was gone. There were too many things she was going to have to settle before she went away. But she could manage it. There were just a few things to settle before she was gone forever.

"They're dangerous," Alice told her. "No one should have them."

Claudia looked more interested as she watched Alice work, like a cat watching a mouse. Alice didn't flinch, knowing full well that she couldn't do much to stop that gaze and having become comfortable with the gazes of cats over the years. She was not quite the mouse they hoped her to be, she found, and she kept working as if she were alone.

"And what makes you think they're so dangerous?" Claudia asked her. It wasn't so much a demand as a question. Alice was in an interrogation and Claudia wanted to know her motivations. "Have you been reading my book?" She paused and continued a moment later, a curious and sneaking grin spreading over her face. "Tell me, have you found more than just the one you stole from me?"

Alice didn't say anything at first, wondering if it had been a mistake to say as much as she already had. It was a delicate dance, and she knew that she had to be wary of revealing how much she knew all at once. "That book is dangerous," she repeated, deciding that she didn't know how much Claudia was aware of already, but she wasn't going to give her anything else to work with using her words because she might be nervous. A mouse should not be nervous when under the gaze of a cat.

"Have you read the book?" she asked again, watching the water start to boil over in the pot. Alice did not sweat, did not break from her work, and turned down the temperature of the element. The house phone rang, but Alice and Claudia both ignored it. There was nothing about that phone that they needed to pay attention to.

"You can stop that," Claudia told Alice as Alice's hand passed back over the sauce, putting a few more petals in. Alice glanced at her and her eyes flashed a sudden shade of grey. It was so quick that Alice wasn't sure she had seen anything at all.

"Do what?" Alice asked, averting her eyes back to the sauce. This conversation was about to take a turn very soon and Alice was already tired dealing with it. She wanted it to be over.

"If you give me the book back, I'll stop trying to find it and that will not be necessary any longer," she told Alice very firmly. "And if you know what's in there, then you know that it's of no use to you. You can't do anything with the information in there."

"I can't," Alice agreed. She had no intention of using anything that was in those books, and she didn't want to know what they were being used for. She only knew what happened to people who read them too much, who delved too deeply and made things with them. And Claudia seemed very much like she was one of those people.

Claudia still watched her, Alice feeling those eyes following her. "And if you can't use it, then what do you want it for?" she asked. "A book is just a book. If you aren't going to use it, then what is the purpose of it?"

"A book is but a book," Alice told her. "And to read a book is to be entertained. And what else is childhood but the constant search for entertainment. And what is growing up, but seeking to find that childhood again when all has stopped being so fanciful."

That stopped them both. Alice felt dizzy and her head was throbbing. She probably needed to sit down. There was nowhere for her to go right now, though, so she turned off the stove and put the spoon down, her eyes glancing back at Claudia.

Claudia was more intrigued than before. She didn't know what to make of the words either, though it seemed clear that she knew there was something wrong with them. Alice knew what was happening. Something was getting through into Wonderland again. Something big had made it in and the madness had slipped through with it. She needed to talk to Tiger Lily and Adam, to see what was going on.

"Alice?"

She caught the look on Claudia's face at the intrusion, the flash of annoyance that she quickly masked as if there was nothing happening there. Alice wasn't about to do anything to dissuade her from that assumption. She would really rather no one knew what they were talking about, or what Alice had just said. She hoped that no one else had heard her, honestly, because she had no explanation for it.

She turned to look at Evan leaning in the door. He cast a wary look at Claudia, then back at Alice, concern crossing his face as he frowned. "Rayne's got the phone," he explained. "Apparently your mom wants to talk to you."

CHAPTER 3

Secrets Kept

CLAUDIA TOOK OVER dinner by means of making sure the stove was completely off and calling for pizza. As Evan led Alice the long way through the house, they could hear Ryan return to bicker with Claudia over whether it was worth it to just eat what had already been made.

"Everything okay?" Evan asked as they walked, his pace slowing. "Lance said something about Claudia doing something while you guys were at school."

Alice shrugged. "It's over now," she said. And it was, as long as she continued to dispel them. At least it sounded like Ryan was winning the fight, given that he was almost done with the pasta.

Just in case, Alice reached into her pocket for another few petals. Her hand disappeared off the end of her wrist, appearing above the sauce and feeling the steam hit it. She dropped the petals in and her hand reappeared where it was supposed to be.

"What did you just do?" he asked, his eyes following her disappearing hand. "Did the Bandersnatch do that to you?"

Alice shook her head. "A tart did that," she told him.

"Where did it go?" Evan asked. "Are you *sure* you're okay?"

Alice didn't meet his eyes. He hadn't asked if she was okay before. She didn't trust where this conversation was heading. "It's just... Claudia did something to them and they're not quite done coming after me."

"Why?"

"I don't know why she's still—"

"Why does she want anything to do with you?" Evan asked firmly, annoyance tinging the edges of his words. "Seriously, you and Rayne."

Alice looked up at him, meeting his eyes. "I don't know."

Evan frowned, but he didn't have anything else to note about Claudia. She would have liked to tell him, but he still lived here. He would have to deal with Claudia day in and out until he went back to school and well after Alice was a problem for anyone. Once she was gone, Claudia would probably go back to normal, and without the book she wouldn't be a threat to anyone.

There was only the sound of their feet padding on the carpet for a moment. Only a moment.

"You haven't dealt with the Bandersnatch," he said.

Alice was already tired of having to tell people. She needed to make a list of people she had to convince, how many people were going to keep asking and reminding her that her end was coming. How many people weren't going to let her enjoy her last days without trying to convince her that she should do something about it.

"I did. He's gone."

Evan stopped and looked down at her. "He's not. You can't lie to me about this one, Alice. I know he's still there."

Alice met his eyes. "He's gone," she told him. "There's nothing to—"

"You can pull one over on Addie, but I can tell when he's still there, Alice," Evan said, jaw set and irritation growing behind his eyes.

Finally, he let out a breath and they started walking again. His shoulders dropped ever so slightly, defeat setting in for now. "Your choice," he said. "Rayne won't even know she should miss you when you go. And I'm not going to tell her or anyone else. *You* should do that."

"Thank you," she said. She hadn't meant to say anything, didn't want to admit that she was lying, but her gratitude slipped out. Lori was doing so well now that she didn't want to ruin anything for her. She should be able to slip away quietly and the universe would continue on without her. No one would know that anything was different.

Well, maybe Evan. Sarah would probably also notice she was gone as well. But Evan barely knew her, and Sarah had other friends that she could fall back on. Neither of them would miss her that much or for very long.

"But if you want to... If you need anything, you know how to get hold of me," he said. He looked ahead and started walking again.

With that, Alice was able to relax next to him, but her mind was back on what was coming. The thoughts circled through her, things she wanted to know but hadn't known how to ask or if to ask. This was not something that she was supposed to be walking willingly into. But if he was willing to answer...

"What was it like?" Alice asked finally. "Being taken by the Bandersnatch?"

Evan looked almost sad when she asked, but that didn't stop him. "Not like much," he told her. "You just kind of wait there. Stuff happens. You see it all. But you don't really know that time is passing after a while. And then you get out and all that time comes back." He blinked. "I didn't like it."

Alice said nothing, turning the explanation over in her

mind. She didn't really know what to make of it, but she knew that it was not as much of a nothing as she had been hoping for. Still, if she didn't know time was passing, it probably wouldn't be that bad. She could spend eternity like that. She more or less had to, really, so it would probably be a fine existence. She wondered if people ever died after they were taken, or if they were stuck as statues forever.

"Your mom might want to call you guys on your cells," he told her as they rounded the corner. "We're thinking about getting rid of the house phone altogether."

The phone was on the wall beside the bathroom, a thing Alice had never noticed before. It was a strange thing, attached to the wall like that, but Lori was sitting under it and playing with the cord as she talked. She looked small now, like she used to when she was deciding if she should defend Alice against their parents. Her head shook in disbelief and her eyes were wide as she stared at the floor.

She didn't need to look up to know Alice was there and waved her closer. Alice sat down next to her as she straightened up against the wall, listening as Lori cut off their mother on the other end. "Hang on, Mom," Lori told her. "Alice is here."

She handed the phone over to Alice, who took it and held it carefully cradled next to her face. "Hello?" she asked, not really sure what Lori's expression was all about. Maybe they had made up, which would be really nice. Alice would really like it if Lori made up with at least one of their parents before she disappeared.

"Hello, Alice," came her mother on the other end. She could hear that familiar strain in her voice like she was trying to hold herself together. She had been yelling or crying and Alice knew it was best to be quiet right now. "How are you? Have you had a good holiday?"

"It's been good," Alice told her. There was a point here, something she wanted to tell her. She doubted it would really matter, but Lori didn't look particularly happy about whatever was going on. She prepared to react to whatever was coming, and to try and appear appropriately upset about it.

Her mother took a breath on the other end of the phone and Alice knew it well. She was going to start talking and maybe for a long time. Alice shifted until she was leaning against Lori and got comfortable. It was taking a very long while to get to it, and she was starting to think that this meant that their mother wasn't doing as well as she hoped.

"You know your father and I are separating," she started, trying to put it more gently than she needed to.

Alice made an affirmative noise and waited for the rest of the words to finally come out.

"Um," her mother continued after a moment. "You know that we just want the very best for you. And we've been working very hard to figure out what we are going to do to make sure this transition is easy for you. That's why we've been letting you stay with your friend for the holidays, so you aren't going to have to deal with all the boring paperwork and everything else that's happening with this."

"Yeah," Alice said. She felt like she was supposed to fill this silence, but she wanted to know what was going on. Giving her mother a chance to go on a tangent was not going to get her any closer to that, but the seconds dragged on as Alice waited for even a sound from her mother on the other side.

Finally, another deep breath on the other end. "Well, we've decided that the best thing for you is to let your father continue covering the costs of your school," she said. "And you'll keep living with him. We don't want you to have to change too much while this is happening, so you're going to be staying with him."

Alice blinked. Well, that was something. Not that it was going to affect her. Her father had controlled her life to this point, so having him continue to do so wasn't anything to be upset about. Even if she wasn't disappearing, she was expecting to go back to her father in the end, back to her old room and the security cameras and the locks on the outside of the door. And to Ms. Miller, who would try to convince her to escape when she was ready to get out of there.

Still, Lori looked upset, so Alice tried her best to look

disappointed by the news. "Okay," she said, and Lori looped an arm around her shoulders.

"I'll be out in New York," her mother continued, clearly trying to keep her composure. "I was offered a job, so I'll be moving out there in mid-January. Whenever you need me, I'll only be a phone call away. You got the cell phone from us this year, right? I'll give you a call as soon as I've settled in. I will always be around and available whenever you need me. And I want you to know I still love you, even if I'm not around anymore. Okay?"

"I love you too," Alice said, her words almost automatic. She knew that was what she was supposed to say, but she wanted to tell her that she had nothing to worry about. Whatever it was she was worried would happen to Alice when she was living with her father, Alice wasn't really going to have to deal with it. She was going to be gone before she got the chance to go back home again.

"I just wanted to let you know myself. I'll let you get back to your friends now. Tell your sister... She knows. Have a good holiday. I love you, Alice."

"Love you too, Mom. Bye."

Lori waited for her to hand back the phone before she caught her in a full hug, apologizing for things she didn't do. "I'm so sorry," she told her. "I thought she would get custody for sure. I don't know why she didn't. She should have."

"What do you mean?" Evan asked. Alice hadn't even noticed he was still standing there.

"Dad got custody of Alice," Lori told him. "She's stuck going back there in the summer."

"You sure your mom would be better?" Evan asked, his face doing nothing to hide his surprise and disapproval. Alice wondered just how much Lori had been telling him about their family. His eyes traveled to Alice as if he was thinking of something to say, but he quickly thought better of it. He knew there was a chance it wouldn't matter who got custody.

"I think Ryan's almost done with dinner," he offered instead. "I'll meet you down there."

Lori helped Alice up, though Alice thought it was more the other way around, and they headed down to dinner, Alice doing what she could to put on a cheerful face. After all, she was happy that everything was settled with her family. She wasn't going to have to deal with whatever it was they were so worried about in the end, and her family would be happy. She wished she hadn't caused them so much trouble, but soon that would be over too.

CHAPTER 4

Expect the Worst

DESPITE THE SUSPICIOUS looks Lori gave her as they said goodbye for the school year, Alice thought it went well. She accepted the noncommittal answer to coming back for spring break this year, and did her best to make it sound like this wasn't the last time she would see her. She made it quicker than she wanted, and got back on the plane with a handful of baked treats as a final gift from Lori. They looked good and Alice noted that Lori appeared to have actually followed the whole recipe this time.

School resumed like the break had never happened. Sarah was watching her carefully, but Alice's neck had largely healed since last semester and she was content to ignore those eyes following her. She was not going to do anything that might make Sarah think that she was going to do anything dangerous, but she did have a nagging sense that she was going to have to talk to her before the end of the year. But that could wait. For now, Alice avoided looking directly at her, even if Sarah did seem intent on keeping a close eye on her.

"So did you go home *at all* over the break?" Heather pressed as they hung out at one of the tables in the common area, snacks spread out across the surface and no books in sight for once, though Robert and Heather had their computers and were working on their own projects during breaks in conversation. "Aren't you supposed to see your family during the holidays?" Even though Heather was completely swamped with homework and her extracurriculars, Alice found that she could always find time to distract herself with other people's business lately. Alice didn't know how she found the time or energy for it.

Alice shrugged. "It was fun," she told her, watching her and daring her to keep pressing. "I got to see my sister. I've spent hardly any time with her in years."

"Yeah," Heather said. She didn't look convinced, but she let the conversation change happen. "How is she?" She had other things she wanted to ask, but was clearly holding herself back.

"Good," Alice said. "Having trouble with Chemistry, but I think she's doing better now. I should ask her how that makeup test went." Frowning, she pulled out her phone and opened it up to send her sister a text, typing out the question.

She knew it would probably be a bit before she got a response, Lori having to work tonight, but it was best to ask.

Her thumb hovered for a moment over the button to send it. She wanted things to be normal, to keep her from worrying. Would she expect a message like this? It might be strange to hear from her again so soon. Not to mention Alice didn't want to keep seeing messages from Lori. It made it harder to deal with not being able to see her again. She deleted the message.

"Hang on," Kevin said, reaching over and plucking the phone out of her hands. "When the hell did you get one of these?" He looked offended about not knowing about it before, but it quickly turned into a smile as he started going through it. "I am getting your number," he told her. "Heather? Rob? You guys want it too?"

"Get her in on the group chat," Robert told him. "Make it easy."

Alice did nothing to protest them passing her phone around. She was barely even used to it yet and she was fine with letting them deal with setting up more of it if they wanted. She already had some things from the holidays, but wasn't in the habit of using it yet.

She finally got her phone back minutes after they were satisfied that she was properly set up and making plans to let Adrianna know they were very disappointed that she hadn't let them know. They were far too excited that they could actually contact her whenever she had gone missing. Which, they noted, she better stop doing or they were going to turn the GPS on so that they could track her down. She wondered if they could actually do that.

"Of course you can," Robert said, passing the phone back to Alice. "If you know what you're doing, you can get all sorts of information out of these."

"Of course you would know," Heather said, grinning. "How's the game coming, anyway?"

Alice tried to look like she was in on the joke, but she wasn't sure why Robert of all of them might know that, or what game she was talking about. For now, she nodded and smiled and stayed quiet, hoping the explanation would appear on its own if she said nothing. If not, she could ask Adrianna when she got back from choir.

"Here, I'll set it up for you," Robert said, taking her phone back and doing something with his computer. Why he had all of those cables and how he knew which one did what, Alice didn't know, but she let him do whatever he needed to do with her phone. "You really should put a password on this," he told her as he typed.

"You're not actually going to track me through my phone, are you?" Alice asked.

"Not unless you disappear again," he said with a wink.

She caught movement out of the corner of her eye, a dark mop of hair talking to his friends as his eyes continued to stray over to her. Right, she had agreed to meet up with Peter tonight and let him continue to teach her to defend herself. She nodded in acknowledgement at him and he jerked his head toward the door.

It was a little early to go, but she didn't really want to be here right now. She needed to talk to Adrianna, to find out what they were talking about. It felt like she should know, and she didn't want them to know she didn't.

Robert unplugged her phone from his computer and handed it back to her. "Here, you can check it out too. Tell me if anything's broken."

"Thanks," she said. She needed an excuse to leave. "I should probably call Lori."

"No one actually uses their phone as a phone, Alice," Sarah told her.

Alice shrugged and gathered up her books before walking away, making a show of pretending to dial the number as she walked back up to her room.

It was surprising to see Adrianna already in the room when she got there. She was at her desk with a book open next to her computer and turned back brightly to Alice. "Hey," she said, her voice already a little hoarse from practice and nursing something to drink.

"Everyone's hanging out downstairs," Alice told her.

Adrianna shook her head, tapping lightly on her desk. "I have to get this done," she said. "It's due tomorrow. First period."

Alice nodded, sinking down onto her bed and putting her phone next to her. Her eyes lingered on it, wondering still about whether or not they would be able to really find her with it. Maybe she didn't want to keep it with her, but that wasn't the only thing she was curious about. "Do you know what's going on with Robert and a game?" she asked.

"Oh!" Adrianna perked up and turned around. "Did he give it to you? He started working on it with the Gaming Club last year and he said it was getting close to done."

Alice nodded but stayed very quiet. That probably made sense. She was pretty sure she knew that Robert was in the Gaming Club. And that he was working on a game. One that could track her with her phone? Or was that just a joke?

Alice put it out of her mind. She could worry about it later. "Hungry?" she asked instead. She took out a container from her desk and offered Adrianna one of the danishes inside. Lori had made her several to take with her, including a few apple ones that she was not very excited about. Over the years, apples came to taste of imprisonment and she didn't really want them anymore.

Adrianna didn't feel the same way and took one, smiling

and thanking her before putting it next to her on her desk. "Are you going back to Wonderland tonight?" she asked.

"I'm meeting with Peter," she told Adrianna, changing into something more comfortable. "He's going to keep teaching me what Tasha's teaching him. Just in case I get ambushed with a shoelace again." Alice laughed at it, though Adrianna looked uncomfortable. She did not find the same humor in what had happened as Alice had.

"We'll never do it again, Alice," she told her. "We didn't even *know*—"

"It's okay," Alice told her. "Claudia wanted her book back. It's fine. Really. It's not like she's going to keep doing it, right?" And just in case she was, she and Peter were both armed with enough flowers to make sure they continued to be dispelled if they started trying to get the book again. "And you guys don't know where the books are anyway, so it's not like you'll ever find them."

Adrianna didn't look happy about it, but Alice wasn't listening anymore. She grabbed a few more of the danishes and put them into a smaller container, hoping that Peter also liked apple. A moment later, Adrianna was left alone in the room to do her homework in peace.

CHAPTER 5

Less Than Helpful

WHEN ALICE APPEARED inside the gym, she found herself alone. She turned the lights on and took a look around at the empty gym, taking in the light scent of sweat that peppered the place. Peter should have let her know that he was going to be a little bit to get there. He could have at least...

Alice tapped her pocket. Right, she had a phone. One that she had left on her bed. She reached out and let her hand disappear off the end of her arm to appear in her room. She grabbed it, drawing it back and starting to go through it. Robert had made a game, right? She could at least give it a shot while she waited for Peter to finally show up.

She had barely loaded it up when a rattling made her stop dead. Her eyes shot up to the windows above the bleachers and to Peter prying one of them open. He must not have the key anymore.

"About time!" Alice told him, though she was smiling about it as she put her phone down next to her. She pulled a black hair tie off of her wrist and tied her blond hair back. A second black elastic followed it to keep her bangs from falling in her face in time for Peter to land in front of her.

Peter made a sour face at her, but grumbled something about one of his friends holding him up. "It's not like I don't want to come, they just don't get that I'm busy," he said, flicking his thumbs across the screen of his phone in rapid succession before tossing it down next to hers. Alice watched as he did it, curious.

It was amazing how quickly Peter adjusted to Lucena Academy since the first time she had seen him. At some point he had not only learned that you don't pick people up and fly them around, but how to use a phone and adjust better to school life than Alice had. He had his own friends now, and didn't need nearly as much help with his homework as he had last year.

She didn't know how he had done it, and she had to admit she was a little jealous. At least she had *seen* a phone before but she didn't get how to make it do the things it was supposed to. Even with Adrianna and her brothers helping — even with Lori trying to pitch in — she didn't know what it was about these things that made them so important. Besides being able to keep in touch with people, she didn't know what the big deal was.

Although, if she was being honest, she liked being unreachable. A phone was going to make that much more difficult.

But she was determined not to be amazed at the ease with which Peter had adjusted from a life in Neverland to a life at Lucena Academy. He was happy where she was still struggling, and that was not something she needed to be concerned with. She was happy for him, very happy, and she would continue to be so. But still, it was suspicious.

"What's that?" Peter asked, noticing the container with the danishes on the bench.

"Lori made snacks if you want something," she told him.

"Lori?"

"My sister."

"Oh," Peter said. He didn't seem that interested anymore. "The one who went missing and found you, right? Kevin told me about it."

Alice wasn't about to correct him, more happy to have her back for the little time she had left and to know she was happy. But they didn't need to talk pleasantries. That wasn't what they were here for. Alice needed to get as much Wonderland stuff done this semester as she could before the Bandersnatch made it impossible for her to do anything anymore, so she had to try and learn as much as she could from Peter to keep her on track. "You want to get started?" she asked.

A grin spread across Peter's face and he swept in at her, Alice falling quickly into the routine. She spent most of her time dodging and getting away, vanishing and reappearing around the gym. When Peter did manage to grab her, she could wriggle her way out of it, but she wasn't happy with just how often he was still able to catch her. She was getting better, though Peter noted that it was very slow progress and he wasn't nearly as happy with it as she was. But he was never happy with slow.

Still, Alice felt more confident. She could get out of more and more of his holds faster, and he was growing frustrated by the ease with which she was vanishing from the air when he was about to get her. Alice even let him try picking up a stick to try and make him feel better as they danced around the gym for the next hour, trying to attack one another. Peter put music on his phone to give them something to listen to, and she was pleasantly surprised to find that they were both sweating when they decided to stop for the night.

"You know, you still suck," Peter told her. He offered her a bottle of water from the recently purchased club fridge, though they didn't have anything to eat. He went through the danishes Alice brought, pocketing an apple while digging into a blueberry one for himself. "I mean, you are *really* bad at this whole thing."

Alice stuck her tongue out playfully at him as she finished the water. "You know, you had years to figure this out," Alice told her. "I haven't always been a hooligan like you were. I have to start somewhere."

"There's an easier way for you to get good," he told her. "Come on, I don't want to be doing this forever."

Curious, Alice left the container behind on the bleachers and went back to watching as Peter swept up into the air and went back outside. She was gone as well a moment later, stepping and appearing right outside to see where he was going. It was not a good hour for kids to be caught out of bed, but the two of them were not ones who would be caught for what they were doing. Still, Alice felt uncomfortable about slipping out to wander campus while they were supposed to be in their rooms and in bed for the night.

Peter waited exactly long enough for Alice to catch up with him before he went straight into the sky. He was happiest, it seemed, when he was flying and he revelled in every chance he got to soar through the air, even if it was a distraction. Alice was in no hurry and walked along until he decided to dive back down and whip past her toward the forest. "Come on!"

Alice's trust in the situation left her as quickly as Peter did when he dashed into the trees and out of sight. She followed behind him, each step bringing her just close enough to Peter to watch him fly deeper into the woods. "What does this have to do with me getting better?" she asked, her heart sinking as she headed deeper in. She finally stopped when she realized where they were going.

No. He couldn't have. Peter might have tried but…

"Peter, what's going on?" she asked, her heart dropping into her stomach. "Where are you taking me?"

Peter sighed dramatically and turned around in the air to her. "Come *on*," he told her. "I found a way so that you can just be good at all this stuff without having to learn it from me. You can just ask to be as good as me! And when you're that good, then you can go back and just save everything all at once and you'll be done with everything. And then you can save Neverland for me too. It's perfect."

Alice's gaze went deeper into the woods. He did it. He really did it. "How did you find out about him?" she asked, staring hollowly into the darkness. She knew what was there. She'd been avoiding it until she absolutely had to face it. "Peter, what did you do?"

For as adjusted as Peter had become, with Alice he didn't bother even trying to read her. "What are you so scared of?" he asked. "Girls are always so scared of everything. Come on, all you gotta do is make a deal and he'll make everything good. And then he'll give you anything you want. It's how I got so good at all the stuff here. It's weird here, and Kevin didn't want to keep showing me stuff, so I made a deal and now I can do all the stuff I have to for school and everything else. No big deal. Hey!"

But Alice was already gone. It wasn't nothing that he'd done. She didn't want to go yet, didn't want to face him until she was done, but she had to know what Peter had done. Peter was her fault and her problem now. Even if he was Kevin's brother, she had been the one to bring him over and now he had gone and made a deal without knowing what he had done. Even if it meant that she was back here before she was taken by force. She had to know, to make him understand that this wasn't worth the reward that he got out of it. He needed to know that this was a mistake and he couldn't be making deals with strange creatures in the woods.

Within a few steps, Alice was in the lair of the Bander-snatch.

CHAPTER 6

Early Birds

THE JUBJUB BIRDS were starting to cry their horrifying cries as she crossed through the foggy barrier into the Bandersnatch's lair. She didn't want to hear them ever again, didn't even want to *be* here. She would be here forever soon, so why did Peter have to drag her here now?

It was getting shinier in here, she was certain. The floor was so finely polished that she could see herself in it, and so dark that she could also see the stars in the sky dancing in the reflection, watching over her as she started to walk. Her steps squeaked, echoing strangely in what should have just been open air. She knew there was something contained about this place, but she couldn't see it.

To one side, the hoard of things the Bandersnatch collected was getting larger and more ignored. For every person he held here, their worldly possessions were added to the corner like a second museum, now held in shelves made of the same shimmering dark stone as the floor, only to be looked at and not touched.

But her attention and her body went right to the garden. It was not so much a garden than it was a cemetery, a series of statues of people, so many now, who had been taken by the Bandersnatch and kept here until she could find a way to rescue them. Except that rescue was never going to come and she was alright with that. There were a few familiar faces, but she knew none of them, not really. Not well enough to need to save them. She had no loyalty to them and didn't feel the need to set them free. With Sarah coming back, she was good to let the rest of them stay here, forgotten like she would be.

That was, until she saw what Peter had traded. She knew the boy standing there. John did not look like he had done anything willingly. Confusion and fear and betrayal marred every line on his face. She could only imagine what it was that he was thinking when he had been given away. That Peter would trade one of his friends from Neverland to be able to fit in at Lucena Academy was tempting, but it couldn't have actually been worth it.

Her shock turned quickly to sadness and she frowned as she put a hand on John's leg. She would be with him soon enough, really, so at least she would have company. Perhaps, if they were ever able to talk, they could trade stories about

Peter. Or maybe she could find a way to give Peter a chance to set him free before the end of the year. She wasn't going to be able to do it, after all.

She took a moment to look at the rest of the people standing around her, silver statues that she knew were watching. She wasn't saving any of them. She wasn't even trying anymore. She wondered if apologizing to people who couldn't respond was worth anything.

She had no way to make the Bandersnatch leave. It was a rash choice back then, and a deal that meant nothing now. Everyone she wanted to get out of here had left on their own. She was going to vanish for nothing.

There was another face here that she didn't quite know how to handle. The guy that Adrianna had been seeing, Wyatt. He made Adrianna happy, but she didn't know he had ever existed. Nike had gotten away with it, and there would be nothing she could ever do about it.

"I'm sorry," she told him, her words quiet as she looked up at him. He was pretty much the only one she felt bad about, the only one she could make herself feel responsible for.

"I didn't expect to see you so soon, child," came a haunting voice that Alice knew far too well. She wasn't scared this time when the black floor bubbled and four eyes cracked open from the shape that came out of it. She knew the Bandersnatch would be there, but she could hold her fear of him in check for now. He could not collect until she had completely lost this bet, so she was safe for a few more months.

Alice shook her head and frowned. "I wasn't planning on visiting," she told him bluntly. "You made a deal with Peter." She knew it was far too late to try and convince him to take it back. Even if she were willing, she didn't have anything to offer any longer. "You know he's very stupid, right? He didn't know what he was doing."

"I am not discussing my deals with others, child," he told her. "He wanted something and I granted him it. That's all there is to it. But tell me why *you* are here. Have you come up with something for our bet, perhaps?" Amusement dripped from every word as he spoke and it was clear that he thought that she didn't have anything up her sleeve. "Has your spark returned? Do you have a will to live again at last?"

Alice said nothing, her attention turning to the mark in the sky that flew in behind her. His feet hit the stone floor with a light thud and he stared at her, incredulous. "What?" he asked, looking annoyed as he leaned back from her, his hands trailing in front of his body to gesture wildly as he spoke. "Why did you run off like that? I'm supposed to be leading *you* here!"

"You traded John to the Bandersnatch?" she demanded, grabbing him by the wrist to keep him close. "Do you even know what you've *done*? You can't just leave your friends and trade them to the Bandersnatch! Don't you know you shouldn't trust strange creatures in the middle of the forest? Or just *strangers?*"

"What's your problem?" he snapped at her, pulling his arm out of her grip and backing up several steps. "It's fine. John said it was okay. And he's not keeping him, he's just hanging onto him until I'm done here. When I go back to Neverland, then he's going to let him go."

Her eyes were wide as they flew from Peter to the Bandersnatch, unable to keep herself in check. This was all a bit too much right now, and she wasn't watching her words. "You know he's stupid, right?" she demanded again.

The Bandersnatch's eyes narrowed at the corners, looking like he might be smiling if she could see his mouth. He said nothing, didn't even move as he watched her and made it clear what his role in this was. He would linger here, impartial, accepting any deal from anyone who got past the Jubjub birds and proved they were worth his time. If people found him, he would reward them even if they didn't understand the consequences. And if she wanted him to stop, she would have to get rid of him herself.

Peter. Peter was the one who had done the stupid thing. The one who should know better. "You are so stupid! Do you even know what you did?"

"I made a deal!" he told her, though he was still backing

up. He glanced at John, but he wouldn't look at him too long. "It was easy! I just said I wanted to be able to fit in and know how everything worked here and he said that all I had to do was let John stay here. I said I wanted him back when I got out of here and went back to Neverland. He said he'd do it because he liked me. He said I was special."

"You're never going back to Neverland, Peter!" she snapped at him. "You just gave him John forever!"

"I'll go back as soon as you save it," he told her, now looking more confident. "If you're so mad about John being here, then maybe you should get started on saving Neverland so I can go back and take him back with me."

"I'm not saving Neverland for you!" she yelled at him. She didn't know why Peter suddenly looked so alarmed. She might be crying, though that didn't make sense. She wasn't sad, just angry and overwhelmed and desperate to make him understand what an idiot he was in relying on her to solve his problems. "You need to go back there and save it for yourself! I am doing enough with Wonderland and I'm not even going to be able to finish *that!* You can't make me save John too! I already can't find Matt and Adam won't come back and... and..."

She stopped and made herself hold back the rest of what she was feeling under a deep breath. She couldn't break down right now, though she really needed the release. It was going to be alright. This was not her problem in the end, and it was not her problem that Peter was very stupid. When June came around, she would be gone and Peter would have to live with his actions. He would have no one else to talk to about this and he would have no one else to force into saving Neverland for him. It wasn't her problem. Not anymore.

"You know what?" she said, pulling in another tight breath and brushing her face clean of the tears that had leaked out of her. "It's fine. You did this. It's what you have to deal with now. It's up to you to get him out of there."

"I didn't do *anything*, Alice!" he yelled back at her, clearly panicked. "He's just holding him while I'm here! It's fine!"

"You'll figure out something," she said, though more for her own benefit than his. She made herself calm down, made her breaths slower and made herself not be so upset. She didn't need to get mad because it was not her problem. She had not agreed to free his friend on top of everything else, and there was no guarantee that the Bandersnatch would have let him go even if she were able to win. It was out of her hands and she had nothing to do with it.

Peter didn't trust it, but he was soon distracted. The Bandersnatch had been watching carefully and now loomed over Peter. He grew large, the catlike shape that was more like a black hole in space than any real shape in three dimensions, and one that seemed to suck the light in when she looked at him. He regarded Peter with those four white eyes narrowing down at him. Peter noticed only after Alice's eyes went up to the Bandersnatch and he jumped away, not wanting to get too close to Alice but *really* not wanting to be anywhere near the Bandersnatch.

"What really brings you here again, child?" he asked, his voice haunting and with a strange edge to it. Alice was immediately on edge herself, not trusting what was happening here. It was a suspicious tone that sounded like it might turn dangerous. She knew it well from her father, when he was trying to find something for her to be in trouble for. "Are you planning to give me something?"

Peter jumped, but seemed to miss the dangerous edge to the Bandersnatch's tone. "No," he told him, trying to stay calm. He laughed uncomfortably. "I brought Alice to talk to you! She sucks and needs to be better."

"Oh?" he asked in a tone Alice was sure she had never heard him use. He was mocking her. "Has she decided that she wants to make a deal?"

"No deals," Alice told him quickly.

"Do you guys know each other?" Peter asked, finally putting it together. He watched the Bandersnatch as he prowled around them, getting a little too close to Alice. When Alice shrunk away from the monster, Peter's eyes narrowed, desperately trying to understand the connection.

The Bandersnatch went back to linger behind Peter, but his eyes stayed on Alice and all four of them narrowed. "Is this an attempt?" he asked, more teasing than anything else. "It is a very strange one, and a very weak one, Alice child. You are going to have to attempt something more than that if you wish to win our little bet. Or were you thinking that you might see if you could trade this one. One guardian might make me consider extending the deadline until the time you are finished with high school. And I might."

Peter's eyes grew wide at that, but it was clear that he still didn't understand what was happening. He opened his mouth to ask something, but decided that this might be a good moment to stay very quiet.

The Bandersnatch considered Peter a little longer, but Alice was quick to come up with a response. She wasn't sure what he thought she might be doing, but she only wanted to know what Peter had done. Now that she knew, they could go. "As tempting as that is, I think we're done here," Alice said. "Come on, Peter. We're not making any deals today."

"Not even for more time?" the Bandersnatch pressed. He didn't move, letting Alice walk away and his words stayed, lingering in the air as temptation. "You don't have much time left, Alice child. I do anticipate you will make a lovely addition, but I was hoping that there would be more of a challenge. You have not put up much of a fight at all. I had hoped for more."

"I'm sorry to be a disappointment," she said, not daring to turn around as she walked away. She could feel herself shaking and she took one big step, vanishing from the Bandersnatch's lair and appearing in the forest. She was shaking, but she kept walking until she was well away, standing just inside the edge of the forest in sight of the school and trying to catch her breath.

It gave her a few minutes of solitude while Peter flew to catch up to her. He initially flew right past her before he spotted her below. He touched down at her side just out of reach, confusion across his face as he stumbled through his own conclusions. He wanted to know what had just happened, but he was trying to find the words and Alice wasn't about to make that easy for him.

"You were going to trade *me?*" he demanded, not sure where he should start. "What did I ever do to you?"

"*You traded John!*" she snapped back at him. She was surprised how tense and wound up she still was, her emotions raw and she was stressed. Soon. So soon she was doomed, and the Bandersnatch seemed to know it as well as she did. It was only a matter of time and, though she thought she had accepted it, her heart was still racing at the idea of joining the garden herself. "It shouldn't be a big deal if I *did* decide to trade you! I could have gotten more time!"

"More time for *what?*" he demanded back at her. He was frustrated, not knowing what was going on and only that he had apparently done something dangerous that he almost got in deep trouble for. Worse, that he was almost caught up in something that might have cost him considerably.

"It's none of your business," Alice told him. She needed to make sure he stayed quiet about this, to make sure that he didn't get word back to anyone else that she really didn't have this worked out. "Don't go trying to tell anyone about this, Peter. The Bandersnatch is dangerous. If you tell more people, they might come and make more deals with him. And then more people will disappear."

"No one disappeared," Peter said. "John's just being held there."

"All those statues are *people*, Peter," she explained slowly. "Their friends traded them for stuff. And they're never going to be able to get them back. And you're not going to get John back now."

"I will," he insisted. "You just have to save Neverland."

Alice was about to protest, but she knew just how futile it was to try. "I'm going to bed," she told him. "Don't tell anyone about the Bandersnatch. It's only going to make things worse. And you'll never get John back."

She didn't have any more for him than that. She could talk to him again in the morning when she had a better idea of what to say. Her mind was so filled with panic and confusion and worry and the knowledge that she'd done something that she shouldn't have done that it felt like a haze of white noise. She just wanted to end this day, to finish tomorrow, and then spend the weekend in Wonderland. She only had a little time left before she would spend eternity in that garden with no one to remember her and so much still to do.

She was back in her room a moment later, seeing Adrianna had fallen asleep at her desk with half the pastry on the desk next to her. It was strange for Adrianna to fall asleep studying, but in her state, Alice could think nothing of it. She got her into bed, Adrianna not waking up even with Alice clumsily hauling her over to the bed and placing her on top of the sheets. Soon enough, Alice was in bed herself and drifting off to sleep, feeling that it was a small mercy that this day was finally over.

CHAPTER 7

Sleeping In

AT FIRST, ALICE didn't notice anything wrong. She had slept just a little late herself and was quickly trying to put herself together for school that day. She didn't notice Adrianna wasn't at her side, cheerfully trying to get her to hurry up by helping her get her stuff together for the morning. Or that she wasn't there to tell her that Alice really had nothing to worry about and she could get there in an instant if she needed to. Or that she hadn't come over to make sure Alice was awake early enough to avoid this scramble. There were patterns Alice was used to and, while something about the morning seemed off, she thought maybe it was just how late she was.

It wasn't until she was nearly ready, having given up on a shower she so desperately needed from the previous night for an extra helping of deodorant, that she noticed that she was not going to be the latest person for class today.

"Adrianna?" she called, tying her blond hair up and trying to brush her bangs out of the way. The bangs decided that they wanted to land right in her eyes and she gave up. There were more pressing matters.

She went to Adrianna's side, looking at her sleeping. She was still on the covers, laying like someone had just dumped her there. It took a moment for Alice to realize that she had been the one to do that. Gently she shook her shoulder. "Hey, we have to get to class," she said. Adrianna remained firmly asleep.

Frowning, Alice continued to try to get her up. Class wasn't that important to her, though she was tempted to leave Adrianna here to sleep off whatever had her so tired. She might have if Adrianna would at least *do* something when she tried to wake her up.

She wasn't normally so heavy a sleeper. A groan, a mumble before going back to sleep, she usually did something to let Alice know it was okay after a couple light shakes. Alice kept trying to poke and prod her to shake her, but Adrianna wouldn't respond to any of it.

Alice put her hand in front of her mouth to make sure she was breathing. Did the Bandersnatch decide to do something to her as retaliation for Alice being such a terrible person to make a bet against? Logically it didn't make sense, but Alice was panicking.

"*Wake up!*" she yelled at her, not sure what else she should be saying. She was trembling, not sure why or what for. She needed to stay calm. All she needed to do was wake her up. Waking people up was easy. So why was nothing working?

Miss Amanda. That was who they were supposed to go to if there was anything strange that happened. Alice glanced at her watch. It was still early enough that she might still be there.

Sarah was at the door when Alice opened it, pulling her hand back quickly to keep from knocking on Alice. Alice started at the sight of her, not expecting the other blond to be standing there. Clearly she saw the look on Alice's face and moved out of the way, though followed along beside her with worried and curious eyes.

"What's going on?" Sarah asked. She seemed to know there was something off all semester and Alice had made a point to avoid her. But now she appreciated having someone there next to her in case something went wrong. But nothing would go wrong. It would be fine. "Alice, what's happening?"

"She's not waking up," Alice told her, knocking on Miss Amanda's door hard and trying to keep herself from panicking. What happened instead was a severe calm. She became a blank slate, watching the door and barely moving at all, her breathing shallow and she didn't even move enough to draw attention. Sarah was unsettled next to her, but put a hand on her shoulder.

"Adrianna?" Sarah asked.

Alice nodded, short and sharp.

Miss Amanda appeared at the door, the smile on her face fading as soon as she saw the two girls standing there and neither of them looking happy. Sarah was quiet, not sure what else to say as they looked back at her. Miss Amanda asked the two of them what was wrong.

"Adrianna isn't waking up," Alice said. It was more like she was giving a book report, trying to keep herself apart from her panic. "I tried, but she won't wake up."

Miss Amanda wasn't sure what to make of it at first. "If she's not feeling well, then—"

"She's breathing," Alice followed up. She needed her to understand. "But she won't wake up. I tried everything, but she won't wake up."

Miss Amanda considered the words for a long moment, trying to decide on a course of action. "Okay," she said. "You have a phone now, right?" The wheels in her head were turning and she walked past them, back down the hall to their room. They followed. "I'll take over from here, and then if we need you for anything, or if we manage to get her up, I'll send you a text."

Miss Amanda went to the room and quickly ushered Alice back out of there with her backpack and phone, going to Adrianna's side. Alice got a glimpse of her as she closed the door, not sure what to make of the look of curiosity across Miss Amanda's face.

She must know Adrianna wasn't faking it. She didn't have it in her to fake it. She was much too nice, and she would wake up if someone asked her, even her roommate if they were fighting.

Sarah kept Alice moving, staying close by her side and trying to be a steadying influence on her. "Are you okay?" she asked. "I'm sure Miss Amanda will think of something. Maybe she's just really tired."

Alice didn't say anything, her mind very far from wanting to do anything relating to classes. She wanted Adrianna to wake up. She wanted a lot of things, but she knew that she needed to keep continuing like she had been. She had to continue to try and be normal. If she wasn't, then she would be in trouble.

"Alice, do you know what this is?" Sarah asked, the fear now creeping into her voice as she spoke. "Does it have to do with... that?"

"With what?" Alice asked, far too distracted with keeping her thoughts from spiralling too far out of control to follow what Sarah was asking.

"That thing," Sarah pressed, her voice turning to a quiet hiss as she looked around, as if thinking that even mentioning it would bring it back. "You know. The monster in the woods."

"I dealt with that already," Alice told her, knowing the lie and letting it come easily out of her mouth. "He's gone."

Sarah hesitated and fell back half a step as they walked. After a moment, she was back next to Alice and gave her hand a squeeze. "He's still there," she said. "Whatever you tried, it didn't work. Maybe you made him mad and he wanted to get back at you."

"It's already dealt with," Alice repeated firmly. "Really. He's gone."

"He's really not, Alice."

She looked at Sarah and fell silent, keeping her disappointment to herself. Something must happen to people that the Bandersnatch took. Evan knew too, though Alice didn't know how he could. She just had to hope that neither of them told anyone.

Sarah didn't let the silence linger long before her quiet voice broke it. "He's not the only one after you right?" Sarah asked, eyes flickering down to Alice's neck. Even with no scars left behind, Alice wished she had left her hair down.

There was Claudia, of course, but all she wanted was her books back. Doing this to Adrianna wasn't going to do anything to help, and Alice didn't think this was anywhere near personal enough for her to do anything to her own step-daughter.

There was always Wonderland, but they stayed on their

side of the mirror. They didn't know anything about Alice when she was on this side and, besides Tiger Lily and Adam, she doubted any of them were aware that Adrianna was a person they could use to get to her. If they could think in nearly that linear a fashion.

No, it had to be someone on this side, and that left only one option. One she did not want to keep talking about.

"What about Adrianna?" Alice asked. "She might—"

"No one is going after her because *she* did something," Sarah told her bluntly. Panic flooded over her face before she softened and turned sympathetic. "I didn't mean it like that."

Alice didn't say anything in response. She didn't know what it was, and speculation wasn't useful. She needed answers, but maybe there just weren't any. Maybe something normal might have done it. Maybe she was just sick and they could make her better. Maybe it wasn't Alice's fault at all. Reaching into her pocket, she tapped her phone to make sure it was there. She hoped that it would ring soon and Adrianna would be awake.

CHAPTER 8

Interrogation

ALICE SPENT THE morning hoping to see her, running into class late like nothing had been wrong. When first period turned into second and the minutes dragged on, she decided a text was the next best thing and kept tapping her pocket, barely paying any attention to the lecture.

She didn't hear anything until the last bell before lunch rang. Alice nearly jumped out of her seat at the end of class as it rang and she fumbled to see the message. Miss Amanda wanted her to come back to her room to answer a few questions, but she said nothing about Adrianna.

Alice rushed over, Sarah following closely behind her, only to find a lot of people crowding outside the dorm, being kept away as an ambulance prepared to leave. Most wanted to get close enough to see what was going on and trying to figure out who was being taken to the hospital. It was strange that anyone would when they were equipped with a nearly full hospital facility in the dorms already. Alice could still remember being kept in the dorms when she was recovering from drowning. Something had to be very wrong if they were taking Adrianna to the hospital.

Still, Alice tried not to expect the worst. She didn't want the ambulance to be for Adrianna. She had just seen her last night. She went through everything she could think of, from when she left Adrianna to go meet with Peter to this morning. She was asleep when she got back. And still asleep this morning. But she was breathing, so surely she was all right, wasn't she? Nothing should have changed that.

She couldn't tell them where she had gone last night. She would have to come up with something else for that, but her mind was spinning too fast with worry to come up with something right now. She had to hope they wouldn't ask.

"I just need to get books!" Heather ranted as she pulled herself out of the crowd, looking from Alice to Sarah as if one of them could do something. She caught herself, glancing back at the ambulance and trying to keep her temper in check, though remained annoyed. "They decided to shut down the whole thing. Like, sucks for whoever that is, but they don't *need* to keep us out."

"I think they do," Alice said.

Heather's eyes narrowed on her. "Do you know some-thing about this?" she asked.

"I have to go."

"No you—"

Sarah held Heather's arm and kept her in place as Alice left in the opposite direction of the dorms. She didn't want to be seen walking through that. She stepped around the lamp post lining the walkway and vanished. They wanted to meet her in her room and so she appeared back at the bottom of the stairs, finding that there were a few adults, some in police uniforms, sitting around and chatting. Quietly, Alice slipped up the stairs, but there were voices following her up.

"Hey," someone called. "Did you need something?"

"They asked to meet me in my room," Alice said. "I think they're taking my friend away." That seemed to be enough, and the woman walked with her the rest of the way in silence, though Alice could feel them looking at her. Alice took some comfort in not being alone, but she was not looking forward to what was about to happen. Her mind was spinning, looking for a place she might have been if they asked but also won-dering what else she could do. If there was anything that she didn't know that might have led to this happening.

"Alice," Miss Amanda said in greeting. She sat at Alice's desk with another officer looking over their room, trying to decide what to do with what she was seeing. "Please come in. Take a seat. We just want to ask you a few questions."

Miss Amanda got up from the desk and Alice replaced her, looking up at the officer. She was a tall woman with arms larger than Alice's head. She smiled down at Alice and she let out a breath, nodding for Alice to do the same. She wanted Alice to relax, so Alice pretended to relax.

"My name is Officer Grady," the woman said. "I'm just going to ask a few questions about what happened to your roommate. Can you tell me if you've noticed anything strange about Adrianna lately?"

Alice shook her head. She couldn't think of anything that might have been strange about her behaviour lately, though Alice hadn't really been paying attention. "No," Alice told her. "Is she okay?"

"They're going to do everything they can," Officer Grady told her. "We did notice there were a few pills in the washroom with your name on them. Do you know if she had taken any of them?"

Alice shook her head. Her heart was racing, but Officer Grady didn't seem to notice as her eyes continued to crawl over her. "I don't think so," Alice said. She resisted the urge to ask anything else, if she knew what those were for or why Alice had been prescribed them.

"What happened the last time you saw her awake?" she asked. "Do you know how long she's been asleep for?"

Alice shook her head again, trying to put things together again. As little as possible about what she was doing. As much about Adrianna as she knew. "She was awake last night," Alice told her. "I left for a bit and when I got back she was asleep at her desk. So I put her in bed and went to sleep and this morning she wasn't waking up anymore."

She was ready to be asked what she was doing when she left but the question never came. "I think that's everything we need," Officer Grady said. "I'm very sorry about your friend."

Alice nodded looked around the room to Adrianna's bed. Nothing looked different, but it felt different now that she knew she wasn't there. She could hear the ambulance outside as it left, sirens blaring and growing quieter by the second. Soon, there were people walking in and causing far too much noise.

Miss Amanda was talking to her next. "We're not sure what might have done it, but we're not ruling out an environmental factor, so we're going to check you at the hospital as well. The school is going to want to do a check on your room to make sure there's nothing in here that might have caused this so you're safe. It might be a few days, so we're going to see if Sarah and Heather can put you up again, okay?"

Alice nodded. Sarah and Heather would take her in, she knew, though she wasn't really interested in the questions that would come of it. She couldn't tell either of them anything, but they would keep asking. She hoped she could come back to her own room soon.

The Bandersnatch was the one who had probably put Adrianna into this state. She was almost certain of it, since it had happened right as she had gone to see him. He was disappointed she wasn't trying harder and decided to punish her for it. He was the only one who could have done it.

"We can do that later," Miss Amanda said, looking concerned. "I think Adrianna's brothers are going to be coming by shortly. They want to come with you to the hospital."

Alice nodded again. From in the hall, she could hear Heather and Lance talking, Lance sounding like he was in a near panic. Officer Grady slipped out to let Miss Amanda and Alice have a chat while she went down to deal with the louder people who had just shown up downstairs. By this point, Alice assumed that the whole dorm knew it was Adrianna because she could hear Joe and Travis talking to the officers downstairs.

"If you don't want to do this, you don't have to, Alice," Miss Amanda told her. "I know this must all be scary. We're suggesting that you go, but we aren't going to *make* you do it if you don't want to."

"I'll go," Alice said mechanically. Her mind was spinning and she didn't know how to respond to any of this, instead watching Adrianna's bed and trying to think of what she should be doing now. The Bandersnatch usually just took people away, didn't he? And when he did, they were gone, no one remembered them. He didn't put people into comas and send them to the hospital.

Heather was outside her room when Alice left, clearly aware of what was going on. She gave Alice a hug before she said anything, Alice taking it and keeping herself together. She looked at Alice, trying to figure out if there were words to make it better and deciding she was going to try anyway. She opened her mouth to talk, but Alice was faster.

"Can I stay with you guys again? Miss Amanda said that it might be the room and they want me to stay out just to be sure."

"Of course," Heather said. "You don't even have to ask. You can always stay with us. Do they know what happened?"

Alice shook her head as Heather led her downstairs. There were so many people here, and it felt like they were all watching her. "She just didn't wake up this morning," she said, keeping her voice low. "But she was breathing, so it's not... that." And her eyes were closed, so she wasn't missing her heart. Her chest was in one piece and they were trying to figure out what they could. The Queen of Hearts hadn't somehow gotten to her, and Alice wasn't even sure why she was considering the idea. She didn't know what to do, but panicking wasn't going to help her.

Heather kept her arm around her until they were at the final step. Adrianna's brothers were sitting there and talking to the officers. Lance sat on the side, not sure what he should be doing as Travis and Joe took the lead, more Joe than Travis, to try and figure out what was going on and what needed to be done right now. When he saw her, Lance went to her and caught her in a hug.

"What happened?" he asked, not sure what he was looking for as he looked at her. "They said she's just not waking up, but they don't seem to be saying anything else."

"I don't know," Alice said. "She didn't wake up this morning. But she's breathing." Alice felt it was very important to include that. She didn't know what else to put in there. She still had her heart and she didn't seem to be in any pain. She just didn't seem to be waking up at all.

"You just can't catch a break right now," he said, trying to smile. "Find your sister, but then your parents and now this."

Heather stiffened next to her, her expression getting curious as Alice shook her head. "It's not really happening *to* me," Alice corrected. "It's just around me."

"Cursed," he told her, nudging her lightly.

"What happened to your parents?" Heather asked, perking up and very interested all of a sudden.

Lance went stiff, looking back at Alice and then to Heather, his expression some strange mix of sad that Alice didn't care to try and read right now. "You didn't tell them?" he asked, not believing this.

"It's fine," Alice insisted.

Heather kept watching her, expecting an answer. "Alice…"

For a moment it looked like Lance might apologize for saying anything. It didn't last long before his lips pressed tight, jaw set as his head shook ever so slightly. No matter what Alice thought, this was not a secret she should be keeping. "Her parents are getting divorced."

Alice didn't like the look Heather gave her, but she was thankfully not forced to endure it for long. Joe and Travis called them over to head to the hospital before Alice needed to deal with Heather trying to be sympathetic. It was fine, she wouldn't have to deal with it long. And they would be settled with their divorce and happy without her soon enough. She was just glad to have the escape to the hospital and away from people who wanted to help her for a little while.

CHAPTER 9

Plan of Attack

LUCENA ACADEMY HAD Alice's room locked up for the week, though so far they had yet to figure out what it was that had put Adrianna in this coma. So far their tests had been inconclusive, and there was nothing letting them know what had put her under. As near as they could tell, she was in perfect health and had nothing strange in her system. There was sign of brain activity and she seemed to be having pleasant enough dreams. It was just that she would not wake up.

Living with Heather and Sarah was different this time. It was like living with the Cases over Christmas, except much worse. Something about not having Lori around to try and keep the mood light and Alice distracted made it so much more obvious that they were acting strangely. Both of them spoke carefully or not at all, Heather avoiding mentions of her family and wouldn't suggest doing too much that might bring up Adrianna, just in case.

Sarah, on the other hand, kept trying to get Alice alone to ask her about what was happening with Adrianna. Alice let her do it once and once only. She wanted to know if Alice was certain it had nothing to do the Bandersnatch. Even if he wasn't the one behind Adrianna's illness, she knew that Alice's time on her bet was drawing to a close and she had not fulfilled her end yet. She insisted she didn't want Alice to disappear, but Alice couldn't help but feel that Sarah was doing this because she felt she had to more than because she wanted to.

Alice found herself changing her shifts at the library so that she could avoid all of her friends and their pitying looks and uncomfortable questions. Even Kevin wanted to talk to her and she had no answers, so she made sure she wasn't shelving at the same time as he was. At least it was a moment of peace she could stretch into hours by slipping away whenever someone did try to corner her. She only wanted some peace and quiet to think about what she should be doing now.

So far, she had exactly one idea and it was not talking to the Bandersnatch. The last time she was there, he'd put Adrianna into a coma, and she wasn't about to risk angering him again. She wasn't even sure what had done it the first time, though some of his words still echoed in the back of her mind.

It was tempting, she had to admit, to put someone else in the garden to get Adrianna back. But she wouldn't be responsible for anyone else. She had already become responsible for the people currently in there, and she didn't even know who most of them were.

The books probably held the answer, but she wasn't sure which book would do it. She needed to get out of there to somewhere private and she needed to go through the books to try and find something. She had notes upon notes that she spent most of her days trying to work out, but she had been so distracted from people trying to talk to her that she didn't have a chance to look through them.

Heather and Sarah and everyone else had made a point of trying to make sure she was around and had people to lean on. Alice didn't want it. She wanted to try and figure out how to get Adrianna awake again. It had been less than a week, but she already needed to get away from the people who were trying to desperately make sure she was okay.

Unfortunately, even the library couldn't give her a break from people. At least she had a much easier time slipping away in here. She could disappear away behind a bookshelf and lose them well before they managed to catch her. It was as close as she could get to freedom right now, since it seemed like everyone knew what was going on and who she was. The girl with her roommate in a coma.

Thankfully, the rumours about her doing it were squashed quickly by anyone who knew her. She was considered a little strange, but Alice and Adrianna were good friends and Alice had no motive that anyone could figure. Add to that how close she was with Adrianna's brothers and how often she was invited to come with them to see Adrianna at the hospital, she was no longer a suspect to the general public. Better, people around Alice had been able to vouch for her, and they were able to keep her out of the public eye. Now she only had to endure a lot of people wanting to give her sympathetic looks.

But Alice wasn't as alone as she thought today in the library. She was in the middle of the stacks when she realized that Robert had snuck up on her. He knew how to be quiet when he had to be, shuffling closer and standing next to her as she shelved until she realized he was there. He had done it on purpose, and he didn't care if she knew it. And that there was no polite way right now to slip away.

"Hey," he said. "How are you doing?"

Alice shrugged. Just don't give him anything to respond to and he'd leave her alone. She hoped that he had something prepared and that it would all be over soon, but she didn't know what she was in for with Robert. He went from being quiet to rambling and it was never clear which one it would end up being with him. "Okay," she told him, shifting the books in her hands. When the silence stretched on, she started putting the books back again.

"They're worried about you, you know," he told her finally. "Sarah thinks you're avoiding her. Apparently you aren't even there when they wake up."

Alice shrugged again, saying nothing and not even looking at him as she moved further down the stacks. She was happy to leave them to do whatever they wanted, and she was happier being able to avoid talking about her problems with people who didn't need to know all of the details. And Sarah and Heather weren't really letting her do that, though Robert had also been there for the attempts to make sure that Alice stayed social and somewhere they could keep an eye on her.

"It's okay," he continued, following her as she worked. "My parents split up years ago, so if you need to talk about anything, you can. Dad even remarried, so if you have to do that, then I'm there for you for that too. It sucks and you probably don't want to talk about it, and I get it. I'll try to get them off your back about it and leave you alone. But if you ever need anything, I get what you're going through. And you have my number if you don't want to look at me while you vent."

Out of the corner of her eye, she could see Robert smiling. If she were planning on still being around after the end of the year and actually had to deal with the fallout of her parents' divorce, then she would have found some comfort in that. As it was, the divorce was the least of things on her mind. She was never going to see her parents again. There was a chance that with Alice gone her parents might even forget what it was that had broken them up and get back together.

"Thanks," she told him, glancing over for only a moment before snapping her eyes back to the books and the shelves. She shouldn't give him the invitation to talk more. She still wanted to be alone to think. "I don't suppose you know how to get someone out of a coma too."

Robert went quiet at that for a long moment, staying in place as Alice took an experimental step away from him and put another book back on the shelf. "That I don't know," he told her, looking awkward about it. "Are they going to let you back in your room soon at least? You haven't gotten a chance to stay in your own room in a long time, it seems. Like, last semester you spent half of it on the floor with Heather and Sarah too."

"It's fine," she told him.

The silence stretched on between them as she put another book back. Finally, he opened his mouth once more, his words slow and hesitant. "Just... whatever happens, don't go into the woods," he said.

"Okay." Alice took another step and kept walking, and he stayed where he was. She made it around the corner before he thought to follow her, but it was already too late. She put the books down on the trolley on the end of row of shelves and disappeared from the library.

Alice reappeared in her room, finding it just as she had left it except with the beds now made. She wasn't supposed to be back in her room until tomorrow night, but it was devoid of anyone who might catch her. They had collected their samples and were just waiting on lab results to give her the all clear. All she cared about was that the door was locked and no one would think to look for her in here.

She reached into the air, pulling the red book out of the hiding spot in the ceiling and settled down at the desk. She wanted her laptop too, but she could hear someone in the next room and she wasn't sure if they would see her hand appear out of thin air and her laptop vanish, so she left it where it was. She could work with just the red book for now and tried to think of where to even start looking things up.

If the Bandersnatch had put her in the coma, then maybe there was something in one of these books. She knew that Adrianna had been put to sleep and the red book, the book that felt unsettling like it was breathing, was her best bet to figure out just what it would take to wake her up again. Tiger Lily seemed to think it was for healing, and waking up from a coma should be some kind of healing thing.

She started flipping through the book and hoped that the

answer would just come to her. What did you look for when someone had fallen asleep and wouldn't wake up? There had to be something in here that dealt with a coma, but there was no way for her to figure out where in the book would have something like that for her. She might light a candle in a while and see what the other set of writing had to say.

There was something weird about looking at it now. She could barely pay attention to anything written on it, couldn't quite bring herself to do more than quickly skim each page before she felt the urge to look away and do anything else. She made herself concentrate, forced herself to keep flipping through, but it was getting harder and harder as the pages passed. Itching at the back of her mind was the knowledge that the book did not want to be read and it felt almost angry that she would try, though she pressed on.

The minutes stretched on and Alice only grew more annoyed. She was finally doing something. And she was alone without anyone wanting something from her. Hopefully there would be no one looking for her for a while. If only her brain would cooperate. She needed to pay attention, to force herself to read the words on the pages. The more she tried to concentrate, the harder it was to look. She was getting dizzy from the effort, and she couldn't figure out what had changed. Had the Bandersnatch taken her ability to read the books as well?

Finally, Alice set it to the side. She was dizzy and light

headed from staring at it, but there were notes on her laptop as well. At the very least, she should be able to look at those. But she'd left her laptop in a room with people who might notice a lone hand without an arm attached reaching in to grab it out of existence.

They might be busy. They might not even be there. Maybe there was no one there to notice.

Alice reached out and quickly pulled her the laptop in front of her, holding her breath and listening intently for anything. She didn't hear any sound from the next room. Letting out a breath, she turned it on and hoped that meant that no one noticed. When she opened the file and started to read, the same dizziness overcame her, the same feeling that she was not supposed to be doing this. Even on the screen, the words refused to let her read them.

Fine. Back to the books. Somehow, it felt less frustrating to have the book rejecting her ability to comprehend it than the screen and she thought she might be able to force herself to read the pages. This couldn't stop her. She had finally figured out how she could save Adrianna and she couldn't be stopped by not being able to read a book. She needed to find someone who could, but…

She didn't hear the window open behind her, too immersed in studying every page of the book. She found all kinds of remedies for problems and ways to make the

body do what she wanted it to, things that seemed medical in a strange way but also very wrong in a lot of others.
She wasn't sure what some of it meant, but she knew that it
wasn't what she was looking for yet. She thought she might
be getting close, that some of these ideas were almost what
she was looking for and perhaps if she just found a little more
information about it, if the words on the page would stop
resisting her...

"Hey!" came a voice behind her. Alice jumped and nearly
fell out of her chair. She snapped around with a yelp. Peter
floated there, looking pissed off as he brandished a danish.
"What the hell are you trying to do? What did I do to you to
make you try *poison* me?"

Alice stared at him, taking a moment to try and figure
out what was going on. She was pretty sure she hadn't tried to
poison him. Even though Peter lingered a foot off the ground,
looming over her with the pastry in hand, she was pretty sure
he wasn't going to try to attack her. If nothing else, she was
very certain that she was not the one who had done something
wrong.

"I'm sorry?" she asked, half as an apology and half to try
to find out what he was talking about. She was ready to run
if he tried anything, but she didn't know what was going on
yet. She wanted to know why she was running from him if
she had to.

"You tried to poison me!" he repeated, throwing the danish back at her. Alice put her hands up and blocked it, letting it bounce off her and to the ground. He swept closer until he was hovering over her, his dark face flushing and anger in his eyes. She was very tempted to run before he did something, but he kept his hands to himself and started yelling. "I've been *helping* you and you *tried to poison me!*"

Alice looked wide eyed at him, then let her eyes drift down to the pastry on the ground. She recognized it as a danish she had given him days ago back when all this had started, an apple danish that had been made for her by Lori. "That's poisoned?" she asked, now more confused than worried. "But I didn't make it."

"Don't try that with me! I'm not dumb!" he fumed. "You tried to give me something poisonous and who knows what it would have done! Maybe I'd be in a coma like Addie is. They said you did it to her, you know. Some people said that was you."

And like that, something clicked. She looked at the pastry, knowing that they had taken it from the room and checked it out when they took Adrianna away. Maybe they couldn't figure out what things were poisonous like Peter could. He knew when something was amiss without even taking a bite. Alice picked it up, bringing it closer to her face to inspect it.

It couldn't be something so simple, could it? It didn't look strange.

"But Lori made them," she said, drawing it closer to her nose to figure out if she could smell anything weird.

Peter leapt forward and slapped it out of her hands. *"Don't eat it!"* he snapped at her, sweeping it off the ground and chucking it out the window. "Didn't you listen to me? It's *poison*. Why did you try to give it to me?"

"I don't like apple," Alice told him weakly, trying to put things together. "Lori made them. I ate the other ones. But Adrianna ate the apple one. What happens when you eat it?" she asked finally, looking at him. "Does it make you fall asleep?"

Peter looked at her like she had gone crazy, his hands moving through the air incredulously, like he was using them to process her utter stupidity. *"I don't know!"* he yelled at her loudly enough that it was sure to draw attention from anyone who might be in the hall.

But Alice didn't care, her mind continuing to put things together. Lori had given them to her, but Claudia was the one who wanted to get to her. Alice didn't fall asleep yet or fall victim to it, so it must just be the apple ones that were poisoned. It didn't make sense to her, but it did change things. It meant the book must have the answer.

Her mind was spinning and she glanced at the mirror. Her mind was too cluttered with thoughts to put anything else together. She needed help, and there was someone else who knew this book much better than she did.

"I have to go," Alice told him, getting to her feet and going to the mirror. She had to find Tiger Lily. Surely she would have some idea of where to look in it to find a way to dispel a poison and wake Adrianna up. She had to get moving so that she could find her.

"Wait," Peter said, catching Alice by the arm before she could go through it. "It's Wednesday."

Alice pulled her arm away and held the book close in her arms. Peter let her go, watching as the mirror changed into a portrait of Wonderland and Alice stepped through, directly into her least favourite part of the place. A tea party.

CHAPTER 10

Much Needed Release

AS MUCH AS she didn't want to deal with a tea party right now, she could tolerate it one last time. She was ready to be criticised for her manners, for not changing out of her school uniform before arriving, for not drinking the stone cold tea that was likely over steeped and disgusting. She just had to deal with it for a moment before she could move on. Hugging the book close to her chest, she looked around the clearing to see people gathered around the long table. She easily spotted Tiger Lily sitting there and looking like she would take any reason to leave.

Alice hadn't really thought about what exactly she was going to do, but she could handle Wonderland. It occurred to her that it had been over a month since the last time she had been here, and she had probably let the number of hearts they had to return raise to far too high a point, but that was only if they had managed to steal back more. Which she was fairly certain that they had. It was Wonderland and Adam had likely been working on it.

"You are quite a bit more than fashionably late, Alice!" came the Mad Hatter's voice, followed by his hat and himself. He didn't look nearly as annoyed to see her this time, nor was he looking her over with disapproval at her choice of outfit. Instead, he looked strangely pleased. "Though I suppose that's better than not at all. We will allow it just this once, I suppose, and only because it has been so long since you were last here. And for actually deciding to be presentable, for once! Sit, sit!"

Alice glanced behind her, seeing that they had set up a mirror specifically for her to walk through that was being guarded by a very unhappy Jabberwocky. It felt like she was lured to precisely this place.

"I don't want to interrupt," Alice said, not sure what was going on. Her mind was still swimming and she held the book a little tighter in front of her as her eyes searched out Tiger Lily. She looked amused at Alice being in such a predicament and did nothing for the moment, enjoying someone else suffering as much as she was in this place. Alice let the Mad Hatter push her into one of the seats and put himself next to her, pushing a cup of tea that looked like she might actually be able to drink it. "Thank you." She still wasn't going to drink it, not trusting that sour smell coming off of it, but she did loosen her grip on the book.

"I was quite and literally heartless the last time we saw one another, and I must say, I did not like it one bit!" he told her. "I have heard that you are to thank for returning my heart! Although I did not request this service and I do hope you are not expecting payment for your actions."

"I wasn't even going to mention it," Alice told him. She wanted to get out of there, to ask Tiger Lily for information and to try and do what she needed to in order to wake Adrianna up, but the Mad Hatter kept looking at her and waiting for her to say something wrong.

"So she has returned," the Cheshire Cat added, his voice smooth as he settled round Alice's shoulders and crowding her. "But will she stay long enough to actually finish her job this time? She is as reliable as a treacle these days, disappearing and not appearing again until it is much too late. And one day, she plans to never appear at all again. She could be eaten and we would never know."

Alice looked back at him, knowing what he was talking about. "Then maybe you shouldn't rely on me," Alice told him bitterly. "Tell everyone to stop getting their hearts removed and you won't even need me any longer. It should be a simple enough thing for all of you to do. It's a very difficult thing for you to lose, if you know how to guard it properly."

"A guarded heart leads to a life poorly lived, Alice," the Mad Hatter said, though his attention went to Cat soon after. "But Alice would not abandon us. Perhaps an unreliable rude girl, though she is, she has always come back. Much like a cat or a rabbit, who decided that they could just not stay away from Wonderland. And who could stay away? It is a place of greatness that we should all want to protect."

"Until the Queen of Hearts decides that she will no longer tolerate the rudeness of all her subjects," Cat told him. It sounded like this was an argument they had had before, though it was enough for him to crawl off Alice's shoulders and closer to the Mad Hatter. "Or until she decides that it will be her turn forever. It was the time for the White King to take his turn, but I do not see him in charge any longer. I do not even see him here at all. He has always been a coward, though."

"Better a coward than a cat."

Tiger Lily pressed a finger to her lips to tell Alice to be quiet and ushered her away from there. Alice saw the claws coming out as the Cheshire Cat drew closer to the Mad Hatter and decided following was a good idea. She wondered what had happened between the two of them and why they were so mad at one another, but it was not her problem right now. She only needed to get Adrianna to wake up, and once she did that she could figure out what was going on with them.

Alice followed along quietly, stepping away and appearing behind Tiger Lily as she dashed away from the tea party. They said nothing as they escaped, Alice hugging the book close to her. Tiger Lily glanced strangely at it as they went, but she said nothing for a while until they were well away and wouldn't be overheard. Alice knew the Cheshire Cat would follow soon enough but, for right now, she didn't care.

"It has been a very long time, Alice of Wonderland," Tiger Lily said. She slowed down and kept walking, Alice knowing that they were heading back to her home. At least, back in that direction. Tiger Lily kept looking at the book with clear distrust, but she did not mention it yet. "We have been worried."

"It's been busy," Alice told her.

"Adam has said. It seems that you have been reading dangerous things once more."

Alice didn't say anything at first, feeling a little ashamed of bringing the book back. Tiger Lily seemed to know something about what was going on and let her shoulders relax as she walked before changing the subject. "The Mad Hatter has been different since his heart was returned," she told Alice. "And the Cheshire Cat has also become more insufferable. Something strange is happening. It usually happens when you are mentioned."

Alice had a feeling that she knew what was causing it.

The Mad Hatter being nice and the Cheshire Cat being surly made a strange amount of sense. The Cheshire Cat knew that she would be gone soon and that there was very little anyone could do about it. Even Tiger Lily seemed a little cagey about it, but she remained quiet about it so far. Perhaps she had seen the look on Alice's face and kept herself from mentioning anything.

"Why do you have that book with you?" Tiger Lily asked at last. "You should not have brought it back. It is dangerous to keep here."

"I need your help with it," Alice told her. "You read it before. You know more about what's in it than I do. So you might be able to help me figure out how to make it work." She didn't let go of it, and curled her fingers around it, letting a thumb brush over the pages. Asking for help was hard, but she needed to save Adrianna. She needed to find a way out of all of this.

Tiger Lily nodded as they went into the plains, Alice finding it strange that they were not going in the same direction that she was expecting them to go. At some point Tiger Lily had moved herself back to where the rest of her people were, absolving herself of the exile that seemed to be largely self-imposed. She watched as they walked back through to the small village, to the people who gave her a second look but stopped at seeing Alice. It seemed that most of them knew who Alice was, and Alice recognized a couple of them from her last run-in with the Queen of Hearts.

"I've missed a lot," Alice said, looking around and trying to figure out what she was looking at. She stayed a little closer to Tiger Lily, though that did nothing to keep them from looking at her. There was only so much she could deal with at once, and this was too much right now.

"My father decided that he wanted to try and return to our home," she told her. "Not everyone chose to follow him. I am helping where I can, and some of us are staying and attempting to make the best of our new home. And to keep things from coming back across where we can, or letting things go over. It is what we can do for our new home. It is safer here than it is there, even with your Queen of Hearts."

Alice nodded. She couldn't argue with that. She could handle the horrors that Wonderland had turned into, and she hadn't even seen any of the Queen's men in her short time she had been here yet, but she knew that Neverland was a waking nightmare. She had seen zombies as wolves and pirates who were falling apart and had heard that there was someone that they were intending to bring them to. And she had seen the one who had been in charge of the place trade his last friend for a second chance in a new world. It was not a safe place to be, and Alice could not blame anyone for not wanting to go back.

"This way," Tiger Lily told her, guiding the way to where she now lived near the center of the encampment. Alice followed as best she could, wondering why so many of these people were watching and whispering as they passed. They spoke a language she didn't understand, though she had the distinct feeling that it was her and not Tiger Lily being watched as she walked through the place.

It was a comfort that she was eventually allowed inside the tent and away from the eyes. Tiger Lily started a fire for the kettle, though Alice noted that she now had a small fridge in her place. It didn't look like it went with anything else, and it drew her attention immediately. She didn't say anything, but found herself gravitating towards it and finding some comfort in at least that small bit of familiarity in here.

"It needs to be replaced sometimes," Tiger Lily said, watching her as she started to prepare tea, "but it is very useful. We have learned to harvest these and use them for food instead of our old ways. We are adapting to life here as best we can. And it is a better life than we would have now in Neverland. Now, Alice of Wonderland, sit. You are very concerned about something. Have you perhaps thought of a way to make yourself survive this curse that the Bandersnatch has laid on you? I will help in any way I can."

"I'm not here about that," Alice said. She put the book down in front of her.

"You should be," Tiger Lily said, stopping Alice before she could begin. She came over to her, grabbing her by the chin and looking over her face. "You look unwell, Alice of Wonderland. I would not be surprised if you have not slept in a very long time."

Alice pulled away, but she didn't avert her gaze. "I'm fine," she said.

"You are not." Tiger Lily stared at her for a long moment before getting to her feet and busied herself with the fire and preparing tea. "You are holding too much in. I do not know what your life is like in the other place, but I am growing familiar with you. I imagine you have not told anyone there that you will be disappearing soon. A fate like that is too much to deal with alone. It is not good for you. Talking to someone may help. Eventually, you will need to let some of it out."

Alice remained very quiet. She knew better than to start talking. It would not end well. She stayed quiet, watching as Tiger Lily poured a cup of tea to steep and eyes trailing to the flames. If she waited long enough, Tiger Lily would stop and they could get back to the topic at hand.

She came back and set a cup in Alice's hands. She bent down to look Alice in the eye and waited. When neither of them said anything, she got up and went to the door. "I have some things to attend to. You will stay here until I return and we will resume this when I am finished."

Alice didn't watch her go, her eyes trailing back to the dying flames. She held the warm cup in her hands, letting it ground her as the scent of berries and mint floated up to her nose. For a long moment, she stayed just like that and tried to keep herself in check.

She could just leave. Tiger Lily didn't know what she was talking about. She had no idea what was going on or what she needed right now. All she needed was an answer and a way to wake up Adrianna. It was her fault she was in a coma right now, and she needed to get her back before she was taken away.

And she missed her. Especially now. There was so much happening, and Alice had no one else to talk to. The Bandersnatch. Wonderland. Her parents. Her brothers. And now Adrianna. It was all getting to be far too much.

The cup was placed back on the table. Her arms wrapped around her legs and she buried her face in her knees. She did nothing to stop the tears from spilling out over her face or to hold back her quiet sobs.

CHAPTER 11

A Promise Kept

WHEN TIGER LILY got back, she found Alice trying and failing to figure out how to start the fire again. "Sit," she insisted, sending Alice back to her spot on the floor as she made more tea. "You look better. Now, tell me what has brought you here."

"Adrianna is sick," Alice said. She rested a hand on the book, playing with the corner and debating flipping through it one more time. "I can't figure out how to make her better."

Tiger Lily blinked. "People get sick, Alice of Wonderland," she told her, not cruelly but very bluntly.

"She won't wake up," Alice insisted. "It's been almost a week. This book knows how to break those kinds of curses, right? She's sick and this is the book that helps you figure out how to make people better again."

"You have much more important things to worry about

than a sleeping sickness," Tiger Lily reiterated, though more kindly this time as she started to prepare the tea and pour Alice a cup. "You have other healers who can figure out how to help your friend. They will know what to do more than either of us might."

Alice shook her head. "It's a curse," she insisted. "It was meant for me. But it came out of these books, so she should be healed by something in one of these books. I just can't figure out where I'm supposed to be looking in here for cures to sleeping curses. I need your help. You read this book before. Do you know where something like that might be?"

Tiger Lily pressed the cup into Alice's hand and moved the book away from her. "I will try to help as I can," she told her gently, "though I did not spend nearly as much time with the book finding things like that. I wished to find ways to put people back together after they had been taken apart. They are very different things, and the answers may be in a part of the book I am unfamiliar with."

Alice took the tea but didn't drink it, watching instead as Tiger Lily took the book and turned it toward herself, her eyes scanning through it. She looked uncomfortable and like it was the last thing she wanted to touch, but her fingers still lifted the pages and started to turn through them experimentally.

"There is a concern, Alice of Wonderland," she told her. "We have a great need for you, but you have not been here.

We are aware that you may stop coming back." She was choosing her words carefully as Alice let her eyes wander to the fire, watching the flames dance as the cup warmed her hands. "I will help however I can. But you will need to allow me to."

Alice took a breath. "I am allowing you to help," Alice told her. "I need to figure out how to make Adrianna wake up. And I can put some hearts back while I'm here too. I'm sorry I haven't been around much, but I needed to... Things happened. I got distracted and I forgot."

Tiger Lily tried to bend and catch her eyes, but Alice didn't look away from the flames. She reached over and tipped Alice's hands upward, Alice allowing the action and taking a drink of the tea. The warm liquid went through her and warmed the insides that were starting to feel ice cold.

"I will try to find a solution for you, Alice of Wonderland," she told her. "I will take this book back and look for the ways that you may wake someone up once more. But you must tell me, do you intend to free yourself of your own curse?"

Alice shook her head. "There's no way to get out of it," she told Tiger Lily. "He's too powerful. And he has the book that might have actually had the answer. Without the brown book, I don't know how to get him out of there. It's okay, though. Being a statue won't be so bad. Apparently it's like nothing happens and you don't know what time is, so at least I won't be bored for all eternity. And who knows, maybe someone else will take up the bet and they'll win and I'll get to be free again."

She took another breath. She was starting to feel better already. Tiger Lily would be able to figure out a way to get Adrianna free. She wasn't sure why she wasn't able to concentrate looking at the book right now, but the book fought her when she tried to look through it.

"I'm sorry," Alice said, trying and failing to rip her eyes away from the fire. "I'm not going to be able to put many hearts back now. I need to last until the end of the semester, but it's only a few more months. Once that's up, you guys are going to be on your own. But I could get started on that now." She started to get up. "Just tell me where—"

Tiger Lily was on her feet and pushing Alice back down to sit again. "You will not be doing that today, Alice of Wonderland," she told her. "But if you are concerned, you may teach me how to do your magic when you return for your answers. I will become Wonderland's witch in your absence. Until we can find a way to free you once more."

"Thank you," Alice said, her eyes finally leaving the fire. She smiled, knowing that any attempts to try and free her from the Bandersnatch were ultimately futile, but she appreciated the sentiment as well. "But don't hold your breath. I'm going to make a fantastic statue, apparently, and he's not going to want to let me go."

"We will see," Tiger Lily told her. She let the matter drop and glanced at her door. Alice didn't notice anything strange, but Tiger Lily seemed to be waiting for something to come through it. She got up and placed the book on the small fridge, pulling out a meat tart to give to Alice. "You may wish to eat," she told her. "It seems that you have had more on your mind than I realized."

"I'm okay," Alice said, though she took the tart and ate it with the tea. It felt good to have at least a few things falling into place. This Bandersnatch curse was out of her hands, but at least Tiger Lily could help her tie up any loose ends on in Wonderland. "Thank you."

The flap opened behind them as Alice took her second bite of pie. She looked back to see Adam standing there, looking directly at Tiger Lily and not even glancing at Alice. She watched as he went to her, words following him before he even got all the way into the room. He was focused on Tiger Lily and a little frantic, still wearing clothes that were much more Wonderland than anything that Tiger Lily was willing to adorn herself with.

"Why weren't you there?" he demanded. "I got to the tea party and you were just *gone*. The Cheshire Cat and the Mad Hatter are getting into it again, and I could have used a hand keeping the two of them from trying to rip each other apart! I thought we could actually have a plan today! We can't keep having people infighting and you can't keep *vanishing* on these things. I know you hate them, but we *need* to work with Wonderland, Lil."

"The meetings are useless," Tiger Lily told him. "When there is action, then they work together. When there is no movement, they only argue over manners. We will continue to watch their borders and keep them safe from Neverland, but it's up to them to find a way to save their own lands. That means it's up to them to decide that their safety is more important than their manners."

"You just don't get how they work," Adam told her.

"I do not," Tiger Lily agreed. "I don't need to. You don't need to. It's not important for you to try and make their peace for them."

"If I don't, who will?" he asked. "You aren't going to. And we need to keep the peace as much as we can until we can figure out something that we can do without Alice, since she's apparently forgotten about—"

"You should look to your left, Adam," Alice said.

Tiger Lily didn't falter, though Adam nearly jumped when he saw Alice sitting on the floor in front of the fire. Tiger Lily sat back down next to her and watched Adam in his stunned and flustered silence for a long moment.

"You're back!" he said. "Tiger Lily must have told you what's going on."

Alice shook her head. Tiger Lily looked very amused.

"Oh," he said, looking flustered before he frowned at Tiger Lily. He took a seat next to Alice and tried to pull himself together. "Well, the Queen of Hearts has pulled back since before. There hasn't been as much movement, but we also haven't been able to get most of the hearts. It looks like she's going after key hearts rather than all of the hearts like she was trying before, but it means a few people kind of have targets on them. They got the Hare again, but the Mad Hatter's been moving the tea party. We couldn't save Tweedle Dum, and Tweedle Dee got caught trying to rescue the heart himself. And they've come after Tiger Lily a few times now."

"And you," Tiger Lily noted.

"They can't catch me," Adam told her, winking and looking much more confident. "But they are trying. I've been trying to lead them away as much as I can, but it's getting nearly impossible to get close enough to steal any of the hearts back. We need to find a way to get them to come out so we can try and get them back. It's starting to turn into a bit of a siege situation, but they never run out of food, so we're running out of ideas. And the Cheshire Cat won't go in. He just keeps telling us to give up."

"He's a cat," Tiger Lily reminded him. "Cats are not known for their bravery."

Adam shook his head. "But we do have some ideas. And

we have some hearts that can be put back. People aren't walking around with them anymore because the Queen's pulling them in and snatching the hearts back, so it's a bit safer to wander around now, but she is going to make her next attack soon and we need to be ready. She's just trying to pick off the most important people. She has all four knights and the King has had several attempts made on him so far. If not for the tea party and the Mad Hatter having some way of keeping it moving, most of us would have lost everything already." He looked exhausted. "But you're here."

"I am here," Alice said, taking in some of what he was saying. She wasn't going to have to deal with most of this much longer, so she tried not to be too worried that she didn't follow along with most of what he was saying. Instead, looking at him, she remembered he was among the list of things she needed to finish before the end of the semester. "Are you ready to come back yet?"

Adam watched her wide eyed as Alice took another bite of the pie. It was cold, but she appreciated having the nourishment. Adam looked at her like she had just asked him why Wonderland didn't make any sense. "No!" he snapped at her. "Didn't you just hear me? We're in the middle of a situation! People are being picked off! And we can't get to any more hearts right now!"

"So no?" she asked. "There's not much time left. And

when I'm gone, I'm never coming back. It's going to be your last chance out of here."

Adam shook his head, a frustrated breath coming out of him. "I'll come back when I have to and not a minute before," he told her. "There's too much to do here. And you're not going to just disappear. The Bandersnatch can't be that big of a deal. Why don't you just work harder on trying to outsmart him? I'm going to need longer than however long you have left to finish off everything here."

Tiger Lily bristled next to Alice, but Alice ignored her. "I've tried everything I can think of already," Alice said. She felt more calm now, though she could feel that panic building up again. "I'm going to disappear at the end of the semester, whether you want me to or not. You have a family to go back home to, Adam. You need to go back."

"Wonderland still needs me," he told her, growing bitter and almost angry as Alice stayed so calm. He was on his feet, pacing as he shot glares at Alice. Alice stayed seated, perfectly still and watching. "*Someone* needs to actually stay here and work on getting it back in line. This place is going to hell and I need to be here to fix it because the person who is *supposed* to be fixing it keeps leaving! What are we supposed to do when you go off and vanish? You disappearing is going to screw us, so we have to fix everything before you go and screw it all up!"

"I'm sorry I'm going to disappear," she told him. "If it helps, people don't seem to be able to remember the people who the Bandersnatch takes. That's what happened with Evan, remember? So when I go, maybe you won't even know I was ever around, so you won't be mad that I can't be around to help you anymore. And I'm going to teach Tiger Lily how to return the hearts, so you won't even need me around anymore." Alice took a deep breath. "I don't want to disappear. But that's what's going to happen. So I am trying to make sure everything's done before I'm gone."

"If you didn't want to disappear, then maybe you shouldn't do it!" he yelled back at her. "You are the only person who can do half the shit we need right now and you're just going to off and—"

Alice wasn't expecting Adam to drop to the ground like a ragdoll, but she wasn't entirely upset when he did. She didn't enjoy being yelled at. Tiger Lily stood behind him, looking like she was only barely keeping her anger in check, and looking back down at him in disappointment. "He has no excuse for his words," she told Alice. "He has been anxious about the Queen of Hearts, but this is no way to speak to someone."

She shook her head and went to one side of the room, uncovering a mirror and looking back to Alice. "He will keep his word," she told Alice, going back to Adam's side. She picked him up and put him over her shoulder, bringing him to the mirror and letting out a deep sigh. "You are free to go, Alice of Wonderland. I will do what I can to find a cure for your friend and you will be able to return Adam to his family. Do not let him return, no matter how much he will plead with you to do so."

Alice's heart did a strange leap in her chest, not sure what she was feeling. It was something that was done at last. She was going to actually return Adam to his family, which was something that she could finally cross off her list. Even if she couldn't save Wonderland, she could at least bring home one of the Cases.

"Thank you," she told Tiger Lily, holding back tears of relief. "For everything. Really."

Alice turned the mirror back into a portal back to her dorm room. Tiger Lily dumped Adam through the mirror and Alice followed after him, feeling a great weight lift off of her.

CHAPTER 12

Caught in a Lie

WHEN ALICE STEPPED back through the mirror, it was dark and quiet except for a blinking light on her desk. She had left her phone behind before she left and she wasn't quite sure how long she had been gone. The realization that she'd left in the middle of the week was starting to dawn on her and she was going to be in a lot of trouble for missing class. She dreaded knowing just how much trouble, but she still went to her phone. She should know how long she had been gone, at least.

She picked up her phone to find many texts waiting for her, demanding to know where she went, and at least one attempt of someone trying to locate her phone. Alice remembered Robert had said something about that before putting a game on her phone, but ignored that in favour of the date. It was Sunday at 2am, and she had been missing for days. No longer than her weekends, but this was not a weekend.

Another time. She could deal with this in the morning. Appear in Heather and Sarah's room and then pretend like she had always been there. Keep her head down and hope that no one would make a big deal out of her disappearance. For right now, she had an unconscious Case sibling in her room and she needed to try and get him to somewhere that he could be found in the morning that was less suspicious.

Though she ignored the messages from the numbers she knew, she found a few from one she did not. Lance had apparently been trying to contact her as well, which saved her the effort of having to try and figure out how to contact him. She ignored the demands that she return from "over there" and sent him a message.

I got Adam back. We're in my room. Please come get him.

She put the phone back on her desk and didn't wait for a response. It buzzed as soon as she set it down and she left it there.

Adam wasn't wearing anything that was school regulated, but there was a much larger issue here. He was carrying a lot of things in that jacket that he could not hang onto while he was on this side. Either he would use them or someone else might get their hands on them, and she didn't want to deal with suddenly giant peers panicking about outgrowing their classrooms.

Alice removed his jacket, throwing it into the gap in the ceiling that she kept the books in. She could feel the bottles rattling when she went through the pockets of his pants, and she frowned at the crumbs that littered her floor. He was using the shrinking and growing potions and she didn't know if that would have a permanent effect on him or not. She had eaten one treacle tart and been affected forever. He had been playing with dangerous things, and things from the Caterpillar. It was not safe.

Even less safe was what he didn't keep easily accessible. Alice slowly worked through what she could find on his front before turning him over. Meticulously she disarmed him, removing the things hidden up his sleeve and in the many pockets of his shirt and pants one by one. All the small daggers and larger knives and things that must have been heavy to keep on him.

There were more items of food as well, and storage things that might have contained small hearts at one point that were empty now. He had collected items and trinkets, small fans and pipes that Alice didn't understand, but if they were from Wonderland then they probably did something. She took each of them from him and put them all in the storage space, finding that it was soon overflowing with things that she had taken from him.

There was a knock on the door, frantic and quick and sharp, as Alice sat down to check his feet and see what he was hiding in his socks. She got up and went to the door, Adam starting to stir with one boot off of his foot and on the ground next to him. She had gotten most of it, she was sure, so he wouldn't be able to do anything too bad while he was over here.

She debated, but got up to answer the door. This boot hadn't revealed anything, so it was unlikely that he had much hiding in the other. Quietly, she let the door crack open.

"*Where the hell have you been?*" Lance hissed at her, pushing himself into the room and grabbing her by the shoulders. "You've been missing for *days* and no one knows where you went!"

Alice winced at how tightly he was grabbing her. She tried to pull away, but she only brought Lance into the room with her. "I got Adam back," she told him. She kept trying to squirm out, wondering if she should do something that Peter had taught her. Words first. He wasn't possessed and trying to kill her this time. "You're hurting me."

Behind her, Alice heard the shuffle move quickly before she saw the blur of motion that was Adam. He caught Lance by one arm and pulled him off of her, slamming Lance into the door hard enough to seal it shut and shake the wall. "Again?" Adam demanded, shoving Lance a little harder this time. At least he kept his voice down. "I thought they stopped trying to kill you."

Alice could see the difference between the two of them now, Adam having gotten larger in his time in Wonderland. His hair was longer as well, tied back in a small ponytail to keep it out of his face, and his clothes, though loose fitting, didn't hide the muscle he had built from all the running and whatever else he'd been doing while he was in Wonderland.

"They did," Alice told him.

"Hey!" Lance snapped at him, pushing Adam back, but Adam didn't let him go. He was talking to Adam, though his eyes kept drifting to Alice to let her know he was still furious at her. "She has been missing for *days*. No one knew what was going on or where she went! Everyone's been going nuts trying to track her down!"

"I went to Wonderland," Alice told him. "I *always* go to Wonderland."

"*On the weekends!*" he pressed. Adam released his grip on his brother, but kept him back as Alice shrunk away. "People noticed you were gone this time!"

"Peter knew where I was."

"Who is Peter?"

"Pan?" Adam asked, confusion on his face as he completely let his brother go. "Is Peter Pan out here?"

"Alice, you don't get to disappear like that!" Lance continued. Adam held him back from getting too close to her.

Alice knew that if she reacted it would always end badly. She stayed still and let him yell at her, waiting for her turn to say anything and trying to decide what she could say to make it any better. She needed to placate him to make him stop being so loud, at least. He was going to wake up Heather and Sarah. "I brought Adam back," she said again. "I'm sorry I disappeared. I won't do it again. If you keep yelling, you're going to wake everyone up."

Lance fumed looking at her, but she didn't move. He wasn't remotely placated by her words, but he stopped yelling. Adam kept himself between the two of them and Alice remained where she was. She wanted to run away before anyone got even madder at her, but she knew that wasn't going to do much right now. She had gotten Adam back. One thing was done and didn't need to weigh on her mind anymore. Finally, she had gotten another one of them back.

Lance finally relented and ran a hand through his hair, leaning back into the door and taking in a breath. "Why did you even do it?" he asked, his volume coming down. "You're usually a lot more careful about this stuff."

"I thought there was a way to help Adrianna," she told

him. "Tiger Lily's worked with the red book more than I have. And I... I don't know why, but I can't read it right now. So I went to ask her if she could find the cure to wake her up."

"Wait," Adam said, bristling as the words came out. "What happened to Addie?"

Lance looked wide eyed at Alice, pointing at Adam. She shook her head.

"I— Of course you didn't," Lance took a breath and returned his attention to his brother. "We don't know. One day, she just doesn't wake up. She's still alive," he added quickly, and Alice could only imagine the look at that had flashed across Adam's face. "She's just sleeping. In a coma. There's brain activity, but the doctors don't know why she's not waking up. It's like she's just dreaming."

Adam rounded on Alice this time, and Lance was quick to grab him and hold him back. "You could have just told me that!" he snapped at her. "You didn't have to get Tiger Lily to knock me out and... Why am I only wearing one shoe?" he asked, suddenly realizing his state. "Alice, where's my stuff?"

"You don't need it anymore," Alice told him. "You can't go around shrinking and growing while you're in school."

Adam tore his hand free and started patting his pockets down, feeling for everything that Alice had already removed from him. He pulled out something from his remaining boot and Alice was quick, her hand appearing above his and pulling the vial away before putting it in the hiding spot and keeping it away from him.

He looked dangerous as he tried to advance on her. Lance kept a grip on his arm and kept him from getting too close. "Alice," Adam said, his voice as threatening as his look. "Where's my stuff? I need it."

"Not here," Alice told him again.

"I'm not staying here," Adam insisted. "There's too much that needs to be done. And it's not like anyone out here is missing me much, right?"

Lance developed a strange look on his face, considering but playful at the same time. "You know, it's almost a shame there's no Bandersnatch anymore. If there were, we could just trade Adam for Addie. It would be like nothing happened at all."

Alice froze in that moment, watching as Adam's look shifted to an murderous one. "Take me back."

Alice shook her head. She should run. She needed a place to run to.

"You said you only had a few months left," he said. "That there was *no way* for you to get rid of him. But now you're telling me he's *already gone?* Take me back right now."

There was a strange look on Lance's face now as well. "You did get rid of him, right?" he asked. "You said..." But Alice could tell that he was having trouble believing it now.

She couldn't stay here. Adam was about to pounce on her and Lance was already loosening his grip on his brother. Alice turned away and vanished from the room, just as there was a pounding on the door.

THE AIR WAS warm, but the rain still sprinkled down on her. She didn't care anymore, just grateful for the chance to be alone and away from everything. She needed to breathe, but the breaths would not come as she tried to force them into her lungs. She was panicking and she knew it. At least she could get away.

She just wanted to get Adam back. To do everything she could before she disappeared forever. She was just trying to make as many things right as she could manage before she was gone. She didn't think it would be this hard to keep herself together. She just wanted to have a nice final semester with friends and try not to get too into anything so that she could enjoy it.

But Adrianna was sick, and it was her fault. And she had gotten Adam back, but he was mad and wanted to return to Wonderland. And now they were going to find out that she had lied about the Bandersnatch and try to make her keep fighting it when she had no way out. She didn't know what else she *could* do, and she was happy enough to disappear with as many loose ends tied up as she could. They didn't understand that this was all she could do.

At least Lori would be happy. And maybe Tiger Lily could find a cure for Adrianna before Alice was gone. Without Alice, maybe Tiger Lily could convince the Cheshire Cat to pass the information along.

And she wasn't going to have to deal with them being mad at her. Not for long. She would be gone soon and that would be the end of it.

She didn't know when she started crying. She had already done this once tonight. There was no point in doing it again, but the tears wouldn't stop. They mixed with the rain on her face, and she did nothing to get under cover as the rain started to come down harder. She sat at the small table on the strange little rooftop garden in the middle of the night and let the tears come, taking her time alone and trying to collect herself.

She was alone in this. She didn't have anyone to turn to, and the only person she had who would listen to her without trying to figure out if she was lying was currently in a coma. She missed Adrianna. She just wanted to enjoy one last semester with her friends, but the end of it was getting closer and closer and it seemed like there had been no time for fun between everything.

And soon, none of this was going to matter anymore.

Alice was soon cold, and she could think of only one thing

she wanted to do. She needed to talk to someone, even if that someone wouldn't talk back. Soaked and upset, Alice stepped away from the roof and went to find Adrianna in her hospital room on the other side of the city.

CHAPTER 13

Act of Kindness

COUNSELING SESSIONS WERE considerably differ-
ent than going to see the psychiatrists in the past. Mostly,
the woman she had been assigned to, Dr. Aliya, wanted to
know what she was thinking and generally trying to make
sure she was alright. There was no trying to reinforce where
the line between fiction and reality was, no threatening her,
no prescribing her medication. She reminded her of the few
scattered people who she had seen between the longer-term
doctors who wanted to make sure she was of sound mind and
doing fine at home. She seemed nice, but Alice still didn't
trust her.

But she still knew how to work her well enough. Her
father wasn't happy that Dr. Aliya wouldn't allow him to inter-
view her personally first, but there were other things that her
parents were concerned about. Her father didn't talk to Alice

at all, but her mother called a couple times. It was strange to hear her mother so concerned, though she knew most parents would be concerned that their daughter had disappeared for days only to be found at the bedside of a sick friend in a hospital an hour away. There was plenty of concern going around but, with her home life in shambles, she was to stay at school so she wouldn't have to deal with what was turning out to be a rocky divorce involving far more than just figuring out custody.

If the school had to call about her again, though, her father threatened to take her back immediately and send her to one of his doctors who could actually deal with her. Or so her mother told her.

Her friends had tried to go back to normal as much as they could. Robert seemed to have said something, giving her a knowing nod when she decided to finally join them one evening. They were more willing to give Alice a pass on hanging out if she wasn't feeling up to it and tried not to make her talk too much. Kevin kept looking at her like he knew or suspected something, but Robert was quick to nudge him quiet. Sarah was bursting to ask her questions, but every time she got too close, Alice made a quick to escape to her room.

The counseling sessions were daily, which meant she couldn't escape to Wonderland in the same way that she used to on the weekends. They were annoying more than anything. She could divert the topic to something else, and they were always perfectly pleased to let her ramble on about anything that she allowed herself to be interested in. She took to bringing in homework so that they could help her with that, saying that she was concerned about falling behind with everything else and they indulged her.

But one Tuesday night a week later, Dr. Aliya sent a message saying that she had the night off the next day. With that knowledge, she texted Peter, asking if he was up for another session. She needed to find a way to cancel more of these. She had to get back to Wonderland and start taking care of the last of things before she was gone forever. More than that, she needed to talk to Tiger Lily, to see if she'd learned anything and teach her how to return the hearts.

She said nothing to the others and changed into something she could move more freely in. She went to the empty combat club rooms now that it was after hours, happy to have a distraction.

Alice appeared in the gym and looked up to the window, finding it wasn't open. Peter wasn't here yet. Not bothered, she plugged a pair of headphones into her phone and let music start playing from it as she sat down on the floor. She started to stretch, trying to keep too many thoughts from invading her mind. There was so much to do, but she had to focus on just tonight for now. And then on how she was going to get a whole weekend off from counseling.

She wasn't expecting Peter to grab her by the wrist when he showed up, but it wasn't odd for him to start off with an attack while she wasn't paying attention. She rolled away and twisted out of it, bumping into someone else who grabbed hold of her arm before she looked up to see what was going on. Lance was standing there in front of her, and Adam behind her now hanging onto her arm, not hard but firmly. She tried to pull out and he wouldn't let go.

She stopped fighting and pulled the earbuds out of her ears. "What are you doing in here? It's closed."

"We need to talk," Adam told her.

Alice looked around for some way out, then up as the window opened and Peter slipped in. He saw what was going on and started to drift backward, but Alice was not about to let him get off the hook that easily. "Hey!" she snapped at him. "How did they know I was going to be here?"

Peter rolled his eyes and flew closer. "I'm not going to carry messages for them," he said. "So I just told them we were meeting and they could talk to you themselves."

"I don't want to talk to them, Peter."

"Well, *I'm* not supposed to tell anyone else about the Bandersnatch, right?" he countered. "And they want to know about him, so if *I'm* not supposed to say anything, then *you* gotta tell them about him." He crossed his arms and sat in the air.

Alice frowned, but let herself get brought back to the bleachers. Adam and Lance sat on either side of her and hung onto her to keep her from going anywhere. "We don't want to do this, Alice," Lance told her, his grip not as tight as his brother's, "but you keep running every time we get close."

Alice tugged at her arms, but they wouldn't let her go. She couldn't run. A little compliance for now, maybe, and she would run at the first chance she had. She met none of their eyes, sitting very still and straight and waiting for her chance to get away.

"Apparently the Bandersnatch is still out there," Lance continued. "Why didn't you just say something? We could help you try to figure out how to get out of this."

"I'm not trading anyone," Alice told him firmly. "And I've already tried everything. I lost a book to him. I can't even read the other ones anymore. There's no way to get out of this. I'm just going to disappear at the end of the semester and there's nothing anyone can do about it."

"Wonderland is screwed if you give up," Adam told her. Lance shot him a fierce look over her, but Alice wasn't bothered.

"I wanted to try and clean up as much as I could," she told him. "I was going to go every weekend, try to put all the hearts back and help as much as I could. I'm going to teach Tiger Lily to put hearts back the next time I'm over there, if I can figure out how to get out of the counseling for a weekend. Wonderland can have her saving it. Or it can find someone else. It made me go back already. Maybe it'll pick you next if it likes you. It will be fine without me. Really."

"You can't just *give up*, Alice."

"There's nothing left to do," she told him, looking pointedly down at both the hands keeping her in place. She should try to do something about it but, as she looked at Peter, she knew that he wasn't going to be of any help to her. And running apparently meant that they were just going to find her again and she would have to do this all over again. If she wanted them to leave her alone to deal with the last few loose ends and do something else to enjoy her final days, then she was going to have to think of something. "I've already tried everything. And now I need to try and figure out how to wake up Adrianna so that everything is okay with her before I can't come back anymore."

"They already have a neurologist," Adam told her. He had been adjusting to life in the school poorly so far, finding himself antsy at having to stay behind a desk and largely spending his time in and out of counseling sessions and assessments to figure out where he should be placed. He was frustrated, but he didn't have any way back to Wonderland and he was still mad about it. "You don't need to solve this one. You can just focus on trying to kick the monster's ass and winning this bet."

"It was Claudia, though," she told him. "It wasn't something normal. Somehow, Claudia did it."

Adam let her go and, for an instant, she thought she could run. Instead, he reached over and smacked Lance upside the head. Lance's eyes clouded over and cleared at the hit, realizing that it wasn't what he seemed to think it was. Claudia's influence was still over him, but he was okay. "What do you mean Claudia did it?" Adam pressed, returning his hand to her wrist.

"I let her eat some of the danishes that Lori gave me," Alice said. "Claudia must have made them. Lori's baking sucks."

Peter nodded next to them and looked very cross about it. "And she tried to give them to *me!*" he added. "And then she tried to eat it herself."

"I was *not* going to eat it," she told him darkly. "But I think Claudia was trying to do it to me, but she got Adrianna instead. It's my fault, but I can fix it. I just need to check the other books for a cure. Tiger Lily is looking at one now."

"Why are you making Tiger Lily do it?"

Alice shuffled and tried to pull herself away from them again, but neither of them moved. "I can't read the books anymore," Alice told them. "I don't know why."

"*Because they were all poisoned!*" Peter snapped at her, flying up in the air and expanding to his full size as his arms and legs flew out wide from him. "You ate the poisoned fruit things! How are you so *stupid* when you keep calling me stupid?"

"How was I supposed to know that?" Alice yelled back at him, snapping at last and pulling herself away from the two of them out of sheer surprise. "I don't know what poison tastes like or smells like or anything! Do you think I'm *trying* to let all of this stuff happen? You think I wanted Adrianna to go into a coma or that Wonderland is going to keep falling apart without me? Do you know how hard I've been trying to get Adam to get back here and he kept *running* whenever I tried? And people keep losing their hearts and you keep thinking that I'm going to save Neverland too, but I can barely figure out what to do with Wonderland and... And I'm not even going to be *alive* in a few months! I should just be worrying about my parents' divorce, but I'm never going to see them again! Lori's graduating and I can't be there for that and I..."

Alice took in a breath and stopped. Tears stung her eyes and she could barely see. She needed to go. She said too much.

SHE RAN, DISAPPEARING and reappearing a few steps at a time. She wasn't sure where she was going, but she needed to think of something. Her path was sporadic, just needing to move and get away.

When she stopped, she was exhausted and sat down on the ground, looking around at where she was. She made it deep into the woods at the late hour, her phone left behind in the gym, and she stayed on the damp ground for a long moment trying to catch her breath. She didn't normally lose herself like that. Normally she could keep herself under control. She was slipping more than usual, but she knew it was only a little longer. She only needed to keep herself together for a little longer.

"Alice!"

She needed to focus. She took a deep breath and tried to keep her breaths slow and contained. To keep from heaving and crying. She wiped her eyes with her dirty palms, then wiped the dirt off her face with the backs of her hand. She was getting dirt all over herself, and her butt was damp from sitting on the dirt, but she was starting to calm down. Her thoughts were getting quieter and she was able to focus.

"Hey! Alice! Get back here!"

She just had to get back on track. She couldn't keep thinking about the things she couldn't change. She would stop going to the counselors who kept trying to talk to her about the things that were causing her stress, who wanted to ask if school was okay and how she was dealing with her parent's divorce and her roommate having fallen sick. It would be better if she focused on the things she could do instead of trying to think too much about the things outside of her control. That was something they had said, wasn't it? Maybe she could take some of their advice.

And something she could do was help Adrianna. Deep in the woods, there was at least one person she might be able to talk to. Someone who might know what she could do or give her a direction. She didn't want to go back there again, but he couldn't take her yet. Not until their bet was properly done.

Alice considered just giving herself over to the Bandersnatch early. This would be so much easier and over already if she could do that. Maybe she could convince the Bandersnatch to wake Adrianna up if she went early.

But she still needed to teach Tiger Lily. To deal with the books. Maybe if he wouldn't help, she could offer herself in a week and try to wrap everything up quickly.

"Stop!" Peter said, swooping down from the trees and sprawling out in front of her in the air. "Jeez, you run really fast, you know that? You're lucky I'm the best at hide and seek or you might have been able to get away."

"What do you want, Peter?" Alice asked. She was tired, but she had somewhere to be. She started walking, disappearing with the first step and appearing well past him. "I'm busy."

"You were supposed to be learning how to not suck in a fight with *me* tonight," he reminded her. "What else could you possibly have to do now?" He continued to follow her from the air, looking ahead and falling back just a little in the path. "Why are we going this way?" he asked. "I thought you didn't want anything to do with the Bandersnatch. You said he was dangerous and I was stupid for making a deal with him."

"I'm going for information, not to make a deal," Alice said.

Peter kept following her. "I'm not going to stay if you ask me to," Peter told her. "I don't want to be a statue. John said he was okay with it. He said he would do it so long as I came back for him later. I'm not doing anything if you're just going to end up in there later anyway."

"I'm not making a deal," she repeated, hearing the cries of the Jubjub birds starting to pierce the air at the sound of their voices carrying. "Quiet. Move quick. They'll start screaming if you're too loud or they see you."

"I *know* that!" Peter hissed, though he spoke more from experience than anything else.

Alice didn't stick around any longer than that, disappearing from her spot and appearing inside the Bandersnatch's lair. He was nowhere in sight, though Alice could already feel those four eyes watching her. She would regret this in the morning, she knew, though right now she was more terrified that something was about to happen. But it couldn't. She had time. She was safe from him until the very end, and free to come and go as she wanted. She was supposed to be sending him back to Wonderland, after all. She was safe, even if she could swear those statues were all looking at her.

"You have been accepting gifts from unfortunate people, child," came the smooth voice as the Bandersnatch appeared next to her, towering over her with his eyes narrowed suspiciously on her. He was like a very large bear today, though the shape of him still showed none of the details of what he actually was. Still, Alice was almost certain that she was being smelled and the Bandersnatch did not like her scent. Peter flew in above her but stopped in the air, holding fast as the Bandersnatch wove around her and Alice stayed perfectly still. "You should be much more discerning. These have given you quite the handicap in our little game."

"Adrianna is sick," Alice told him, keeping her voice solid and strong though the fear was creeping up in the way her heart pounded. Still, she tried to keep herself calm, kept herself from reacting to the fear so that it would not overtake her like the rest of her emotions kept doing.

"I am aware," he said, stepping back from her and giving her some room. He started to walk, and Alice knew he expected her to follow him out of the garden. She did as she was meant to, Peter drifting down to stand and walk next to her as well, though he looked uneasy. "A tricky curse. Much like the one that you currently possess. The same resolution for them both, however."

"Is it just that flower again?" Peter asked.

The Bandersnatch laughed and it was an entirely cruel sound that sent a chill through Alice. Peter faltered and shrank next to her. "Alice is not incorrect about you," the Bandersnatch told him. He sat in his throne and watched the two of them before him, so small as he towered over them. "It is not so simple as a flower. I don't think the books will help you with this."

Alice didn't like the sound of that, but she said nothing as Peter shifted next to her, already itching to open his mouth again. Alice didn't stop him, knowing that at least she was safe and hoping he could fly fast enough if the Bandersnatch got mad.

"So are you going to tell us how to fix it or what?" he asked. "Or is Alice stuck not being able to do anything and you're just going to make her wait until you take her away forever? It's not like she can even *try* anything while she's poisoned like this."

The Bandersnatch looked amused, getting up from his throne just enough to sniff Alice again. His eyes narrowed and Alice wondered if that rumbling she was hearing around them was a growl. "It does interfere with our little bet, doesn't it?" he mused, though Alice wondered what was really happening here. He pounced off the pedestal and snaked around both of them before facing them, his four eyes all directly on Alice.

"You will be mine soon enough, but I expect you to make a better show of things."

"If you'll help save Adrianna, I'll do whatever you ask," Alice told him.

He didn't seem to believe her, but he continued anyway, eyes narrowing on her. "You have already given up, but you will not be permitted your placation for long," he told her. "I do not wish to win, child. I wish for a challenge. And you will provide me one or I will find one elsewhere. Though I will enjoy taking you if that's what you want."

Alice said nothing, not sure what the threat was. Instead she stood silent next to Peter, who was very uncomfortable. She remembered how confident he was when they came the first time, but it didn't matter now. She waited, watching the Bandersnatch. She wouldn't flinch as he watched her.

Finally, he sat back. "You will need Pendragon to wake her."

Alice blinked. She wasn't sure what he was talking about or what it was, but it sounded like it was something that she could find easily enough. It was a dragon. She needed to find a dragon, or at least a dragon thing, to wake up Adrianna. It was, at least, a goal. "Where can I find that?"

"Neverland. Near the black book." He stood up and looked back at Peter, Peter shrinking under his gaze. "You will find it," he said, though Alice wasn't sure who that was directed to. He stalked away, leaving them in the darkness of his lair with the feeling that they were being watched still.

"We should go," Peter said, pulling her arm and trying to pull her back and away.

Alice wanted to ask what it was, but the Bandersnatch wasn't even looking at her anymore, back at his garden to admire the statues he'd collected. She opened her mouth to ask more, to at least know what it was, but Peter kept pulling her back and away. Her body didn't protest, the pounding in her chest agreeing well with the impulse in her feet to get out of there.

Find the Pendragon near the black book in Neverland. She could do that. She had heard of the black book plenty at this point, so it was only so long before she could find it. She had a direction, and she could probably figure this out. And so she followed Peter's lead and the two of them walked out of there.

"Find Pendragon and many of your troubles will be solved," The Bandersnatch promised as they left, his voice following them out. "If nothing else, you should become much more interesting."

Chapter 14

Adjusting Plans

ADRIANNA'S SEAT WASN'T empty in class anymore, though Alice wasn't sure about the Case that replaced her. Adam didn't look annoyed or frustrated by the work given to them. He was annoyed that he was here at all, and sitting next to Alice didn't help matters. She served as a constant reminder of where he could be right now, and he very pointedly did not talk to her unless he had to.

She didn't know what he was so mad about. He wasn't the one who was trying to bring back his sister on a deadline. But at least she had some idea of what was going on now, and someone she could ask for information. All she needed was a lot of time, and spring break was coming up. She could head over and take care of everything at once.

Adam, for his part, had decided to be honest about where he had been when he was asked, almost seeming to delight in how Alice winced and made her hasty exit when he started talking about stealing hearts and fighting knights. No one believed a word he said, but Alice was still not happy with how freely he talked about it.

"No really," Heather insisted as they settled in for studying one night. "You were gone for *years*. Where the hell were you?" Heather was happy to have him back, taking a seat next to him to help him catch up.

Adam pondered for a moment, shooting a look at Alice before he continued. "Stealing hearts," he said again, winking.

Alice was very small, still, and quiet next to him. She couldn't say anything now, couldn't warn him that only bad things came out of talking about Wonderland. He didn't care and continued to talk about it like he wasn't going to be sent to the doctors for it. So far he hadn't been, and Alice was starting to think he never would be. Everyone around him seemed to take his words as a joke, though Alice's heart raced every time he mentioned it. And she was sure he was doing it on purpose.

"At some point you're going to have to tell us what really happened."

Adam looked offended. "Are you saying you don't believe me?" he asked, aghast. "I took orders from a madman in a top hat and fought human sized playing cards. I got kidnapped by birds and this is the thanks I get."

Alice wanted to point out that no one had asked him to do any of it, but she held her tongue as the people around her, her friends, assumed it was all a joke. It was for the best. Better that they didn't think he had lost his mind and gone mad in his time away. The school had tried to get something out of him, as had his parents, but his father was unable to come up with anything about his whereabouts and didn't seem that concerned about it. He just said that he knew that he would show up again and that was that.

So long as he didn't mention her, Alice decided. If he did get hauled away, she didn't want to go with him. She only had a little bit of time left as it was, and she didn't want it cut any shorter. She had to make this semester last long enough to wake up Adrianna.

"You're going to get in trouble talking about it," she muttered when there was a lull, the conversation drifting to a class that Adam wasn't in.

"Take me back and you won't have to deal with me."

"You'll never come back if I do."

"I'll risk it."

Alice glared back at him, but she was done here. She didn't have the energy to keep working on her homework. She got to her feet and went off, spotting Peter by the door and deciding it was time to start putting a few plans into action. Spring break was coming up and there were quite a few things that she needed to do before she went over there. Like find out just what she was in for in Neverland.

Peter was gone by the time she came back, but she knew Peter's backpack now very well. She reached out and grabbed the red handle of it, appearing behind him and holding it as he snapped around.

He tossed the backpack off his back. They were not alone in the hall, but no one seemed to notice that Alice had just appeared from nowhere. If people weren't going to notice she could appear from thin air, then maybe she could do it more often.

"What are you doing?" he demanded, looking around and snatching his bag from her. He shrugged it back on, eyes wide as they stared at her. "What do you want?"

"I want to know about that book," she told him calmly. They started walking and Alice fell in step beside him, the two of them heading to the rooftop garden. Peter had learned it was a safe enough place, and Alice was more than happy to go as well. "He said I needed to find Pendragon and it was beside the black book. In Neverland."

"You know," Peter said, "she might wake up on her own. You probably don't need to do any of this."

Alice shook her head. "I need to know about the book, Peter. And where it is. Wendy has it, right? And you know who Wendy is and where she would be. And I don't know Neverland at all. I need your help."

"I'm not going back there," he told her as they walked closer to the theatre. His footsteps were getting lighter, his feet starting to leave the ground already. Alice put a gentle hand on his shoulder to keep him grounded for just a little longer, no matter how he might want to fly. His footsteps were quick, like he wanted to get away, but he knew Alice could catch him no matter where he was. "You can't make me go back there."

"I just need to know where to go," she told him. "A map or something. I mean, backup would be good too, but if you could maybe just go back and drop something where she is, then that's all I need. Just a little thing, anything I know so I can find it and I'll do the rest of it myself."

"Are you seriously thinking about going there alone?"

Alice stopped and turned, looking around for where that voice had come from. She knew it was Adam, but she thought she had removed anything that might have helped him do Wonderland things while he was out here. He was nowhere in sight, not that she could tell, and she wondered what she had missed.

"Adam?" she asked. "Where are you?"

"Look up," he told her. She looked above her and saw that he was on the trellis on the side of the building, using no

Wonderland magic and yet still not making a sound to alert her to his presence. He had learned a lot, it seemed, in his time in Wonderland, and Alice was not pleased about it. He dropped down next to them from far too high a height and shook his head at her. "You can't really be thinking of going there on your own."

Alice didn't need to stand for this, so she stepped back and vanished. She appeared in the rooftop garden, sitting at one of the seats and letting out a sigh. "Hey Peter!" she yelled into the air, not bothering to hide her location.

Peter flew over to her a few moments later, though he didn't look happy about what was happening. "He's right," he told her. "You shouldn't go alone. And I'm not going to tell you where to go. You're not going to make it back."

"I'm not going to be around much longer anyway," Alice insisted. "I don't know anything else I can do. It will be fine. I can just disappear whenever something bad happens, right? Maybe carry a mirror around so I can get back to Wonderland. It will be fine."

"Is there a mirror big enough for you?" he asked, tilting his head sideways to look at her. "You *are* getting smaller, though.

"She's not eating," Adam said. He had scaled the side of the building and now threw himself over the roof and into the garden. "Your friends noticed," he added to Alice. "Kevin also thinks you might be dating his brother. Don't worry, I told him that was a hard no."

"I need to go, Adam," she told him. "It might be a chance to save Adrianna."

"How about you do something to try and save yourself?" he suggested bitterly. "You're walking into a death sentence if you go into Neverland on your own."

"I'm disappearing soon anyway," Alice countered. "It's fine, it just means I go sooner than later. Or it means I get out and bring this Pendragon thing with me and then I can save Adrianna before I go. The Bandersnatch said that it would cure both of us of curses. Maybe it will help me figure out how to get the Bandersnatch while I'm at it."

"Do you really think that?" he asked, clearly not ready to believe her.

Alice shrugged. "I don't have any other options," she told him.

Adam looked her over carefully. "What are you looking for?" he asked. "What's a Pendragon?"

Alice didn't know and shrugged. "He said it was by the black book," Alice said. "And that's all I found out before Peter decided we should go."

"So you're looking for Wendy," Adam said. "Wendy's the one with the book. And she's in the old oak. You're going to need someone to take you there." Adam looked at her seriously. "And you're going to need someone to watch your back while you're in there. Wendy is not as soft as the Queen of Hearts. You're not going to just get your heart ripped out. I know that doesn't sound as bad, but you don't recover from what Wendy does to you. It's not Wonderland."

"I'll be fine," Alice insisted. "I just need to know where it is. Someone should be able to help me. I thought Peter might, but apparently not."

"Someone else," Peter muttered helplessly. "It's someone else's turn."

Adam looked at him, but his attention was still focused on Alice. "You know this is a death trap," he told her. "You walk into there and you don't walk out. Wonderland is screwed, Addie is screwed, everything is screwed if you're gone."

"I'm going to be gone soon anyway," she reminded him again. "It's time everyone figures out what to do with themselves when I'm not here anymore. Besides, I still need to go over there to see if I can find Matt. I wanted to try and save all of you before I was gone. I don't think I can, but I want to try."

A growl emanated from inside Adam's throat and he looked like he was going to tear into her again. His hand darted out as he walked past, grabbing her by the shoulder and holding her in her seat. "No more disappearing, Alice," she told her. "You can't just keep running from everything.

All this stuff isn't going to go away just because you aren't here anymore."

"You won't even remember me when I'm gone."

"That isn't the point!" he snapped at her, Alice letting out a small yelp as he squeezed her shoulder hard. She didn't move and he didn't let her go. "You need to at least try to not get yourself killed out there, Alice. We can all see you *now* and we're worried you're going to get yourself into something that you can't get yourself out of. And it looks like you are."

Alice stayed very calm, remembering that Peter had showed her how to deal with this. She looked at Peter, who was backing away and looked worried about what he was looking at. He was not going to help her. And if he wasn't going to help her, then she was going to have to help herself.

She reached up and grabbed Adam by the thumb, turning around so that she could tear it backwards. Adam jumped and let her go, letting out a cry of pain. Alice took the opening and jumped away, disappearing from her spot and appearing at the very edge of the garden. "Don't come back here," she told him. "And I'm never taking you back."

She vanished, looking for somewhere else she could have some solitude. If Peter wasn't going to help her, then she would look elsewhere. It would be fine. She had spring break and when that happened she could be gone for as long as she needed to be. And soon she would be gone for good. It was fine. It would all be fine.

CHAPTER 15

Movie Night

IT SHOULD HAVE been easy. As soon as class got out, spring break would be upon them and Alice could slip out before anyone knew she was gone. It was a full week without counseling, so she didn't have to worry about getting prematurely kicked out and taken away by the Bandersnatch while she was gone. There was a bag waiting for her with a change of clothes and everything in her room. She thought it would be enough to walk out of class and head right for her room and a mirror. It should have been that simple, if she wasn't currently sharing a desk with Adam Case.

"So," he said, draping an arm around her shoulders and holding her back as Heather made her way over. "What are you doing tonight? Any plans? Going anywhere fun?"

Alice glared at him. He knew perfectly well where she was going and she tried to shrug him off of her, but he wouldn't let her go. Heather stopped at their desk and looked pleased with herself and with him. "Hey, you caught her before she disappeared!" she said, keeping her tone light and like she hadn't been planning this. "You are hanging out with us tonight."

"I am?" Alice asked. "I was going to get started on—"

"Even *I'm* not getting started on homework tonight," Heather said, cutting her off as she hooked an arm through Alice's and started to pull her out to the halls. "We're going to hang out. See off everyone who's going away with movies and pizza. And you're coming."

"Really, I was just going to—"

"Going where?" Adam asked, amused and knowing full well where she was going. "Were you going to take us up on the offer to come home with us? Because that's still open, even without Addie. And we don't leave until tomorrow, so you can still make tonight."

Heather looked at him for a moment in a look that Alice recognized. She still wasn't sure about why the family was going back to the other coast when Adrianna was in a hospital over here, but she said nothing. After Adam returned without saying just where he had been the past couple years, nothing that anyone believed anyway, she was starting to accept that there was just something strange about that family. Worse, they still didn't react to questions about Matt. Her attention was back to Alice soon enough. "Anyway, you're coming with. Right now."

"You don't really need me there," Alice tried, though she was met with Heather's derisive noises and shaking of her head.

"We really don't," she told her bluntly, though hugged her arm tighter in an attempt at comfort. "You've been getting more distant and ghosting us like crazy this semester. And I get it, you're dealing with a lot right now. But you're not the only one dealing with stuff. Adrianna's friends with the rest of us too. And we were following along with the saga of the missing sister." She knocked gently into Alice's side. "You don't actually have to do this alone, but you're making it really hard to be there for you."

"I'm sorry."

Heather made an annoyed sound and loosened her grip, content that Alice was no longer about to run at any moment. Part of that was only because Adam looked ready to pounce if she did. "This isn't an apology thing, Alice," she told her gently. "But you always do this. Something stresses you out and you don't talk to anyone. You know you can talk about anything with us, right?"

"Except during finals."

Heather's face cracked into a smile. "Except during finals. Then you talk to Rob. He's not going to pass anyway."

"You two are terrible to your friends," Adam said as they made their way into one of the movie rooms to find there were already people there.

Lance and Kevin were discussing something quietly in the room while Sarah and Robert were debating over the selection of movies. Alice noticed Peter was absent, though she wasn't surprised. Peter had avoided her since their last encounter.

"It seems like something must have happened," Kevin said, his voice not quiet enough to not be heard at the door. "Are you sure—"

"She's *not*," Adam and Lance both told him firmly, Adam smiling as his brother looked up to see him. "Unless," he continued, looking back at Alice. "Hey, you haven't been going out with Peter while we weren't paying attention, have you?"

"No?"

"There you go."

Kevin flushed red and turned his attention to the movies, leaving Lance to join the argument over which one first. Sarah and Robert were arguing loudly over a fantasy movie, Sarah insisting that it was going to put people to sleep while Robert suggested it might be a good thing for her then. Kevin was quick to step in and mediate, refusing to look back.

"So you actually caught her," Lance said, looking from Adam to Heather.

"You doubted me?" Heather asked, grinning. She tugged

Alice over to join in the debate for the movies. "Come on. Pizza. Movies. *Fun*. Oh, but first," she added, stopping Alice halfway across the room. "I was thinking, since I'm going to be here for the break too, did you want to room together?"

Alice shifted. "I mean, if you want," she said. Heather was far too close to say no. "Aren't you going to be busy studying and stuff though?"

"Doesn't mean I couldn't use the company."

Alice smiled, though her expression was hollow as she did so. "Sure," she said. "We'll figure it out in the morning?"

Heather smiled and let her go, following her as they settled in. Alice happily kept her mouth full of pizza and let the conversations happen around her, slowly accepting that she would still be able to go, if only a few hours later. And given she didn't hold very high hopes of seeing any of them again after this, she might as well let herself relax for a couple hours.

Listening, though, made her wonder just how she had missed so much happening in her friends' lives. She had been too immersed in her upcoming disappearance to know that Robert had been seeing another girl in their class for about a week. Or that Kevin had been receiving what looked like fan mail, but he would not divulge why. Or that Sarah had been trying to convince Adam and Heather to just go out already since he got back.

It was better when the movie started. She didn't feel so guilty about not paying attention to the things happening around her or to the people she thought she cared about. Alice stayed quiet as they ridiculed the movie, delighting in the comical eighties gore and ridiculous premise.

Sarah leaned in next to her part way through the second movie. Alice wasn't sure when she'd moved next to her, but it didn't much matter now. If she wanted to talk, this might be her last chance.

"Maybe the boring one would have been better," Sarah suggested. "I'm never going to sleep after this."

"Have you been sleeping?" Alice asked.

Sarah shook her head and moved the empty pizza box from the chair next to her onto the floor. "It's okay," she told Alice, keeping her voice very low. "I'm getting a lot of stuff done. It's just... those eyes, you know?"

They were both quiet for a long moment while Alice waited.

"He's still there," Sarah said.

Alice nodded. She let out a breath, watching another stream of blood fly across the screen. She knew it was coming, but she still didn't know how to respond to it. Sarah knew somehow, and she couldn't convince her otherwise.

"What was it like?" Alice asked finally. "Being a statue?"

"It wasn't really *like* anything," Sarah said, though her

body was tense and her voice was barely audible over the movie. "You just kind of... aren't for a while. I didn't know how much time was passing until I got out. And you get to walk around sometimes. It's not so bad until you see him eat. But at least he doesn't do that very much."

A chill ran through her when Sarah went quiet, staring at the screen and seeing nothing of what was happening on it. Not hearing the laughter as someone made a comment about the stupidity of the characters. Part of Alice wanted to ask what she meant by that. She hadn't thought about what the Bandersnatch must be eating, but she also didn't want to find out.

"But I saw you coming in and out," Sarah said finally, her voice a little stronger. "Heard you trying to get us out. Heard about that bet. You're going to be gone soon, aren't you?"

Alice stayed very quiet, trying not to say anything. She kept her eyes on the movie, but her mind was on what was coming. On the Bandersnatch. "No one will even know I'm gone," she said.

"I think I'll remember you," Sarah said. "I asked Heather about Wyatt. Lance too. None of them know who I'm talking about. Kevin almost did once, though. You know who he is."

"That guy Adrianna liked," Alice said. Sarah relaxed next to her and leaned against her. "Nike traded him."

Sarah let out a soft laugh. "He wanted a blond hotter than

you to make you jealous," she said. "He was really pissed at you for cheating on him. With Kevin, but that's stupid. He's gay."

"What?"

Sarah shook her head. "He hasn't said anything, but it's obvious, isn't it?"

Neither of them said anything. Alice wasn't sure if they were still watching the same movie. It seemed like the scene had been going on forever, fluctuating between screaming and heavy breathing and the laughter in the room as someone shouted something at the screen. Sarah let out a breath and rested her head on Alice's shoulder.

"No one will be mad that you didn't get them out," Sarah said. She sounded tired. "It wasn't fair."

"It was fair," Alice said. "I just failed."

"I'll miss you when you're gone. Even if no one else remembers."

Alice was quiet, but she had to say something. She felt like she had to. "I'm sorry," she said.

"Did he do it to Adrianna?"

"No, it wasn't him."

"Good. Stay away from him."

Alice looked at her, but she had drifted off to sleep. "I'm sorry," she said, the words quiet and sad as she looked back at the movie. She wasn't watching it anymore, heart too heavy and guilt weighing on her. She knew what she was leaving behind, knew that she wouldn't be quite as forgotten as she thought. And somehow, that only made her feel worse.

She had to go. Now.

Gingerly, she took Sarah's head off of her shoulder and laid her down. She looked so tired and Alice was not about to make her wake up if she could help it. Alice had already done enough to her, and she was about to do even more. If she couldn't get the Pendragon...

She might come back. There was a chance she would be back.

Alice ducked around the back of the chairs and vanished up to her dorm. The light was already on when she appeared, and she wasn't alone. Sitting on her bed and looking through her school bag, Lance was already waiting for her. He looked up, expression mixed and brows knit.

"You don't have to go alone, Alice," Lance told her. "Or at all."

"It's to save Adrianna," she told him. She reached up and her hand disappeared off the end of her wrist. When she pulled her hand back down, it was back along with a second bag fully packed for her trip. "It's my fault. I need to try and wake her up before I'm gone."

"Do it later," Lance told her. He started to get to her feet, but stopped when Alice stepped toward the mirror. He sat back down slowly, hands out in front of him like he was trying to keep her calm. "Come back with us. At least see Rayne again. Lori."

Alice shook her head. "She won't even remember me when I'm gone. Tell Heather I'm sorry, though. It would have been fun."

"Do you at least have a plan?"

"Find this Pendragon that can wake her up," Alice said. "Bring it back."

"And if you can't find it?"

"Make a deal." She looked at the mirror and it was already reflecting Wonderland back at her. He didn't need to know that she might not make it out of Neverland. He didn't need to know what the deal was. This was keeping her. "I'm sorry. I have to go."

Lance lurched forward and tried to grab her, but it was too late. She stepped through her wardrobe mirror and she was already in Wonderland before he got to his feet.

CHAPTER 16

Loose Ends

ALICE FOUND A secluded spot to change as soon as she got over. She put on much more comfortable clothing, shoes, and Adam's coat with all its pockets, weapons, and far too many mysterious mushroom-based concoctions. She hoped some of it would come in handy while she was in Neverland. It was big on her and very heavy, but it was her best chance of coming out of it alive. She would much rather be a statue where someone might someday rescue her than be killed in a land that wasn't even after her heart or telling her she was rude.

The stupidest way to find Tiger Lily was the only one she could think of. Alice reached out and grabbed hold of the handle of Tiger Lily's knife and brought herself to it. As soon as Tiger Lily felt the tug, she grabbed her wrist and Alice's back flew into the ground, the knife in her hand pressing to her throat. Tiger Lily loomed above her, ready to let it sink into her skin if she decided she didn't like the person trying to steal from her. Alice let out a grunt as the air left her lungs, wheezing the air back in and trying to placate her with a weak smile.

"Alice of Wonderland," she said, getting off of her and offering her a hand up. She smiled and pulled her to her feet. "You know better than to try and steal from me. I am sorry to say I have no answers or any more information from the book. It does not have much about people falling into deep sleeps, strangely. Mostly just if a physical injury takes place."

Alice coughed and shook her head, trying to wave her quiet as she looked around. They were not far from her village, standing in a forest of trees with fridges hanging off of them in various states of ripeness. It was a strange thing to think of, but she suspected that Tiger Lily had to regularly harvest them now these were a source of food for her people.

"I'm not looking for that," Alice told her. "I need a few favors."

Tiger Lily regarded her, but nodded and looked around. There was a small fridge that she had already cut down and she put it onto her back before looking at Alice. She considered it, then set it down between the two of them. "Bring this back to my tent," she told Alice. "We will speak there."

Tiger Lily waited until Alice nodded before she took off

in a run. Alice put her hands on the fridge and tried to pick it up, but it was much too large for her to carry. She didn't know how Tiger Lily did it, though the fact that she had more muscle than anything else on her was likely something. Alice managed to get it just barely off the ground and took a step, appearing in her tent and dropping it as soon as she was there.

Alice dropped down next to it and took off the coat and bag. Both were far heavier than she thought and they dropped to the ground with consecutive thuds. They were in no rush, but it would be easier if she had as much settled as she could before they started moving.

One by one, she drew the books out of her bag. Every journal and story she had written about her time in Wonderland was stacked on the fridge, Alice straightening them out of habit. Next to them, she put the green book.

The jacket was next. She didn't think she would need to, but it was much too heavy for her and she needed to leave some of it behind. There were things to eat in here, things that would change her in size and things that she wasn't sure what they did, but she hoped they would keep her alive. If not, she hoped they would not fall into the wrong hands. A Neverland person with Wonderland food could probably cause more trouble than anyone was ready to deal with.

There were weapons in here too, and she removed them. She didn't know how to use a knife or any of these other things. She was only probably going to hurt herself carrying these, or let someone take them from her and have them armed while she was trapped. She left them in a small pile by the fridge. When she put the jacket back on, it was light enough for her to move in, if too big.

She pulled a fan out of the pocket, remembering the weight of it. It was the White Rabbit's fan, and she wondered if she could use it to just shrink it a little bit so it would fit her better.

Tiger Lily appeared and Alice pocketed the fan once more. It was only for a little longer. She could handle it.

"Why do I feel like you are going to ask me to do things I will not like, Alice of Wonderland?" Tiger Lily asked. Her eyes looked around the room, at the knives and weapons on the ground and the books piled on the fridge. She kept her expression light, though she moved quickly to start making tea. "You are going to test the limits of what I am willing to do for you. Is that Adam's coat?"

"He doesn't need it anymore," Alice said as she took her seat on the floor. There were chairs and a table if she wanted it, but Alice was not a fan of that particular table or those chairs, not after the last time she had been forced to use them. The red book spread open on the desk was not helping matters.

Alice carefully didn't look at them and took a deep breath

as Tiger Lily passed her a cup. She opened the fridge, but Alice declined anything to eat, trying to work out the words she needed.

"I have a few things to ask," Alice told her. Tiger Lily would probably turn her down if she gave her the choice. She should have just left it all here with a note instead, but she needed to settle all of this before they left. Tiger Lily had to take her.

Tea. She had tea and she took a drink of it to calm her nerves. "The books," she started. "I need someone to look after them when I'm gone. When the Bandersnatch takes me, there's someone else who wants them, and I don't think she's going to do good things with them. She's the one who put Adrianna into the coma, and she's the one who made everyone go weird last time." Alice made a face and drank her tea. Her words were getting away from her. They were doing that a lot these days. "She can't get them, and I don't think she can get here. But no one else can get them either."

"I will keep them safe until you return," Tiger Lily told her.

"The rest are mine," Alice told her. "It's everything that's happened in Wonderland. The first time, and all the times after. Everything that might be important or related to anything that I've seen or done in Wonderland. And some of the stuff outside of Wonderland. It's got stuff about the Bandersnatch and the Jabberwocky and everything. I just..." Alice faltered, trying to find the right words. "I think you might be able to use them to find Matt. I thought of everything I could, but I must have missed something. You might be able to see something I couldn't. And if you find Matt, maybe find another way to get him back home."

"If I can find him," Tiger Lily said. "He has been much more difficult to find than we expected. I brought Adam into Neverland once on his insistence, thinking that perhaps he might be able to find his brother. He did not. And Adam learned why we avoid going back to Neverland. Not that it stopped him."

Alice suddenly felt much better about putting Adam back on that side of the mirror. She eyed the rest of the weaponry that she had pulled out of the jacket, wondering just how much of it was there because of his excursions to Neverland. It was an unsettling thing, thinking of how often he might have gone that he needed to carry this much on him. She wondered about what he could do now, of how large he had gotten, and how much of it had been just from Wonderland's issues and how much had been from Neverland.

"This all seems too simple, Alice of Wonderland," Tiger Lily said at her silence.

"And I need you to take me to Wendy," Alice told her. She didn't meet her eyes, not wanting to see the look that came across her face at the request. The urge to say no, she knew, was there, and she caught it as she looked up. Tiger Lily's face didn't bother to hide it, though her lips stayed still as she watched Alice and waited for an explanation.

"There's something in Neverland," Alice told her. "It's going to wake up Adrianna. Something called a Pendragon? I need to go and get it before the Bandersnatch gets me. He said it was by the black book, and that's where Wendy is. So I have to go there."

"It is a dangerous task, Alice of Wonderland." She watched Alice for a long time, waiting for her to relent, but Alice held her gaze and didn't look away. Finally, Tiger Lily sighed and shook her head. "For you, Alice of Wonderland. But you know it is dangerous. You may not return."

Alice nodded. "I know. That's why I'll teach you to put the hearts back before we go. I'll show you now. The White Rabbit has people and their hearts, right?"

Tiger Lily's expression soured. "Cat will be there. He is insufferable."

Alice nodded. "He is. But you wanted to learn."

"Then we will go," Tiger Lily said, leading the way out. She offered her a smile. "I almost dread this more than Neverland, Alice of Wonderland. Almost."

CHAPTER 17

Educational Detour

ALICE WAS NEVER sure why the White Rabbit continued to allow his house to be taken over by people in their states of heartlessness before. Now that she saw a heartless young man with a head that looked a little off tending to the garden, she was starting to understand. The flowers were in full bloom, and the various people who had been buried to their necks were growing overshadowed by the flowers that were only just starting to develop faces. They chattered without saying much, and Alice was quick to walk past to the door before any of them figured out how to grow eyes.

The door was open ever so slightly, so she moved to let herself in. Tiger Lily held her back, nodding inside to the voices clearly in the midst of something. It seemed that there was a meeting happening, but Alice was not that concerned about intruding. She was used to being considered rude. Even knocking first would have been rude, just as much as letting herself in. She shrugged and pressed on.

"And I have told you, I am quite uninterested in pursuing a task any greater than managing my garden, thank you very much," the White Rabbit said. "My flowers are growing quite well now, and I have all the hands I need. I do not need to have any more. In fact, I daresay I could do with a few less!"

"I daresay you *should* have a few less!" the Mad Hatter said in agreement. "We only ask that you unearth some of those hands so that we may find some new hearts for them! Why, once they have hearts restored to them, they will surely be so grateful that they will pledge allegiance to the King! And we could greatly use the numbers, let me tell you."

"And how did you think you would make their hearts so persuaded?"

"Why, by speaking directly to their hearts before they are reunited with those pesky brains, of course!" he said. "They will understand if we cut out that bit, and once we have swayed their hearts, their minds will have no choice but to follow! We need all the help we can get, my good Rabbit. You know what it is like to have been taken by that terrible Queen."

"Yes, and I very much do not wish to repeat the experience."

"You are kin with our King," the Mad Hatter said, confused as he regarded him. "I do not know how you could abandon your own in these dire times."

"Kin from a far different game," the White Rabbit told him. "We have been playing chess with a deck of cards for far too long. It is making you forget how things were meant to be. And I was meant to have my reprieve long before now. I served my time and I serve it longer. You will do no good trying to convince me to do even more for you."

"Are we not friends, my good Rabbit?"

"I suppose we are not."

"Allies?"

"Perhaps."

"In knowledge of one another's company?"

"Certainly."

"Then perhaps some arrangements can be made. Perhaps you would allow me to speak to the hearts you hold here."

"Absolutely not," the White Rabbit told him firmly — more firmly than Alice thought she'd ever heard anyone from Wonderland say anything. He glanced over, spotting Alice as she stood quietly in the corner and nodded to her. "I daresay, my good Hatter, I thought you were the rudest of beings in this household, but it seems we have an intruder."

The Mad Hatter flew out sideways, drawing a sword and pointing it directly in Alice's direction. "Have at thee!" he exclaimed, brandishing the sword with far too much expertise and control. "This Rabbit may be a mere acquaintance at this moment, but he has been a dear friend and I will not allow another to have his heart again! *We will not go—* Oh, it's only you, Alice."

Tiger Lily was ready to pounce on him, knives in hand and edging forward. Alice shot her a glare and she stopped her advance, though didn't loosen her grip on her knives.

The Mad Hatter lowered his sword and shook his head, looking very disappointed in Alice. "Returning to your old habits, I see. I would hope even you knew to knock and announce your presence so I would not have to greet you with my blade."

"Perhaps you should not be greeting people with your blade at all," Tiger Lily suggested through clenched teeth. "You have been far too loose with your sword of late, Hatter. One day you will behead someone you do not intend."

Alice kept her hands up until he lowered his sword and let out the breath she had been holding. "I'm just here to put back a few hearts," she said loudly, shooting another glare in Tiger Lily's direction. Of everyone, she was not one to talk about greeting people with a blade to the throat. "Adam told me you were keeping them all here."

"Don't think you'll get to them!" the Mad Hatter cried. "The White Rabbit has decided to lock them up tight so that they may never be harmed again! Taken the choice of bearing their hearts from all these poor creatures, decided that they are not worthy to decide who or what they give themselves to."

"Or just decided that a heart works much better with a brain to decide when to keep it from getting broken," came another silky voice, appearing in the air above the White Rabbit. He looked at the Mad Hatter with disdain. "You would attempt to sway a heart before it could hear or see what it was you proposed. A heart needs a body to understand whatever you may use to attempt to sway it. Otherwise, you will not receive a proper rejection of your proposal to have their heart removed again."

"I will not be subjected to that Cat again!" the Mad Hatter said, brandishing his sword wildly around himself before he set it back under his coat. "I bid you all a day! Good or bad, that is not in my hands and I will not state my wishes!"

He left, slamming the door dramatically behind himself. Alice stared after him, but let him go as the White Rabbit let out a deep sigh. He went to the corner of the room, to a large armoire, and started to fidget with his keys. They clicked and clattered against one another as he struggled to get it in the lock.

A woman came down the stairs, hole in her chest and trash in hand that she brought with her to the back of the small house. Alice noticed now that there were many people milling about, performing household chores without their hearts. She wondered where those from Neverland were, since they were not ones to walk around when they had their hearts removed.

The Cheshire Cat appeared floating at Alice's side. "Like a mouse that thinks that the cat doesn't already have him," he mused at the door. "But they always have hope when they do not know. I have met many a mouse that isn't aware that the end is upon them. They think that the cat will set them free. They think the play is their chance for escape. But once they are caught, they are already at their end."

"Still plenty of time for the mouse to escape," the White Rabbit said dismissively. "Very resourceful, those mice. Even if many of them are missing their hearts. And this mouse has brought a friend."

"One to eat and one to play with," Cat said as he vanished to settle on the couch. "The mouse has given the cat more to enjoy and done nothing to save herself."

"Must they always speak in riddles?" Tiger Lily asked. She put her knives away, but kept her voice low and glared at the Cheshire Cat. "There is no point to them. It would be better to be direct."

"That's not how Wonderland works," Alice told her.

"They are ignoring me."

"And I'm very jealous of you."

The White Rabbit opened the cupboard. She was a little

surprised at the number of hearts that were there waiting for her to put back, but she wasn't concerned about it. It was a good thing. Plenty for her to teach Tiger Lily with.

"Adam was quite busy before you left with him," the White Rabbit told them. "If you could be so kind as to put these all back where they belong, I will forgive your intrusion and allow you a cup of tea perhaps."

"Thank you," Alice said, going in and trying to figure out just how many of these there were to put back. A full drawer of them, so many of those in this house, if they matched. She wasn't sure they would, but with any luck at least a couple would work.

"Mice attempting to escape should not try so hard," the Cheshire Cat put out, still bitter and annoyed in his words. "These hearts will only be removed again. And soon there will be no way to put them back."

"What has you so bitter today?" the White Rabbit asked. "You have been quite out of sorts for a long while, my dear Cat, and not in your usual way."

"She plans to leave," the Cheshire Cat told him. "Leave and never return."

"Wonderland will find someone else," Alice told him bluntly, taking the first of the hearts and trying to decide where they belonged. She handed another to Tiger Lily, frowning as she stared at it. There had to be a way to figure out which one went to whom before starting with the rest of the procedure.

"Give it a squeeze and they'll come," the White Rabbit said.

Alice did as she was asked, as did Tiger Lily. The woman with the trash returned empty handed, looking oddly down at the heart in Alice's hand like she knew it. Beside her, a large badger in a monocle and vest approached Tiger Lily with a similar expression.

"And where will you be going?" the White Rabbit asked.

"I'll be a statue."

"That sounds terribly dull."

"I don't really have a choice."

"Why, there is always a choice. You could not be a statue as well. I daresay, it has been a much more enjoyable experience being not a statue."

"I lost a bet," Alice said. "I will have no choice but to keep my word. I will become a statue."

"You have not lost this bet yet," Tiger Lily noted, looking over the large badger in front of her. "Quiet. Alice of Wonderland has much to teach me."

Alice nodded and held the heart out in front of her. "I'll show you first," Alice said, holding the heart out in front of her. It had been a while since she put one of these back, but this time felt different. Something felt wrong already, but she didn't know why.

The movements came back to her easily, but there was something creeping into her mind as she performed them. Something telling her that she should stop. But she had told Tiger Lily she would teach her. She needed to leave someone else who knew how to do this behind.

"*Ábedecian geángang æþel innoÞ!*"

The words were hard to get out. Her vision went white and she lost track of her directions, not knowing where up or down was, only where the heart in her hand was flying to. Though her body desperately wanted to become a heap, she forced herself to stay on her feet until she was done. When she felt the heart click in place, she and the woman both dropped.

Tiger Lily reached forward and caught her before she hit the ground, her heart forgotten and tumbling away. "Are you okay?" she asked. She didn't wait for an answer before she carried Alice to the couch and placed her next to the Cheshire Cat.

"Do you remember the words?" Alice asked. "Because I don't think I'm going to be able to say them again."

"Explain the rest of what you did, Alice of Wonderland," Tiger Lily said. "You will not do that again."

Slowly, Alice explained everything she was supposed to be doing and Tiger Lily collected the fallen heart to follow the instructions as best she could. Alice's hopes sank as she watched Tiger Lily move the way she was supposed to, watched her concentrate so hard that she broke out into a sweat, watched as she said the words.

Watched as the heart did nothing.

They tried again and again, Alice explaining it in every way that she could. Nothing worked and Alice wondered if it was just her. If there was something about Tiger Lily, that she was too much Neverland and not enough Wonderland to make the spell work.

Or if Alice was the only one who could. If there would be no one else.

"Do not explain again," Tiger Lily eventually snapped at her. "I understand. I will figure this out. Perhaps if I did not have an audience."

"You may use the kitchen," The White Rabbit suggested.

Tiger Lily glared, but she took the badger with her into the other room.

"A very strange bet you made that we're doing this now," the White Rabbit said, taking a seat on Alice's other side. "I have not chosen my successor well at all. Although it appears my dear Cheshire has not done very well in his selection either."

"I am not being sent out to select people! I picked you, and you picked her. It is hardly on my tail if she never stays. She is a stupid mouse."

"A mouse that may escape yet," the White Rabbit said. "She is not lost yet."

"As good as," Cat said.

Alice blinked. Did she hear that right?

"So Wonderland didn't choose me?" she asked. "It was you?"

She got no more answers, instead getting a very cold shoulder and a stern look from a very irate cat. She continued to sit there, staring off at the heartless people of Wonderland tending to the garden and waited. In the other room, she could hear Tiger Lily growing more frustrated with the spell and wondered how long it would be before she gave up.

CHAPTER 18

A Terrible Idea

TIGER LILY KEPT trying until she was almost hoarse. When they finally left, she looked like she would rather be in Neverland than look at another badger ever again. It was clear that the inability to do it wore on her in how tight she held her shoulders and how her face was frozen in a scowl that would not look at Alice as they went to the border between Wonderland and Neverland.

"You will need to come back, Alice of Wonderland," Tiger Lily told her firmly. "I could not return the hearts. You will need to train another."

Alice let out a sigh. "It should be fine," she assured her. "You know how to do it, even if you can't. You know the words and everything else. If anything happens, you can keep teaching more people until someone else can do it."

Tiger Lily clearly didn't believe her, but she let it drop.

"What will you do there?" she asked instead. "What is this Pendragon?"

"I don't know," she admitted. "Something dragon related, I think. I just need to find it and bring it back. I should be in and out of there before anyone even realizes I'm there. You don't have to come all the way with me, I just need to know the way."

Tiger Lily looked like she didn't trust Alice on this one, but she continued beside her until they made it to the tear. "It will be very dangerous. You must stay by my side. We will stop and see my father first. See if he has any advice or knows if she has moved. And if she has, he will know where."

Alice nodded. "Sounds good," she said. "Do you know where your father is?"

"Yes."

Alice heard the tightness in her reaction, but said nothing. They were here and she adjusted Adam's coat on her back, patting the pockets to make sure there were things in there. She didn't know what would be useful, but she had to hope some of it would keep her alive long enough to find the Pendragon.

They went to the part of the tear that peeked out of the top of the hill. It was such a strange hole in the universe, one that was so easy to open up and fall through. She wondered if this was how all holes were, but she knew the mirrors felt very different. And Peter had found his way out by flying into the stars, somehow. Alice wanted to tell him that the stars were much too far to do that, but she knew Wonderland. Things that shouldn't be possible often ended up being far too real in here and she knew not to assume Neverland made any more sense.

"Let's go," she said, leading the way through the crack and remembered very suddenly that she didn't much like the experience at all. There was a stabbing in the back of her mind and she found the darkness of Neverland was quite an irritating change. It was so much darker than the hills that she thought there must be something here to help her adjust. A candle at the very least! It was so unbearably dark that she could barely see the hands in front of... Oh, there they were.

"Come with me," Tiger Lily insisted. She move in the underbrush and away from the barrier and waved Alice to follow her.

Alice frowned and crossed her arms. "Why, I daresay, you should be much more polite if you wish for me to follow!"

Tiger Lily stopped and looked back, shoulders tense as she looked at her. Her eyes were alarmed for only a moment before her body settled into irritation. "*Please* follow me, Alice of Wonderland," she said slowly, doing her best not to raise her voice. "It is dangerous and we must get to safety before any-thing happens. And we must be quiet or we will be found."

She was being very rude, but Alice shook her head and followed at her summoning. She had asked her to show her the way, after all, but it was a terrible thing to be so rudely summoned when she knew full well that Alice had needed her. It was taking advantage of the situation, really, and she didn't appreciate it. "I should write a letter," Alice muttered. "This is most un-nice and uncalled for."

Tiger Lily stayed very quiet, giving Alice nothing to respond to so that she could not continue to tell her just how rude she was being as they approached a small light in the woods. Not a light. A strange patch of trees that looked very much unlike trees. Tiger Lily led the way in and they were soon in the small village, an encampment where Tiger Lily seemed welcome but the presence of Alice earned her nothing but strange stares.

A melodious voice that Alice didn't understand joined them, quiet still but one that was familiar. Tiger Lily's father stood tall above them, towering over his daughter and looking down in some measure of discontent. Except that he spoke in a language that Alice didn't understand. And Alice stared up at him, frowning as he ignored her. Tiger Lily spoke to him in return, speaking in that language that she didn't understand.

On the one hand, Tiger Lily was speaking much more quickly now than she had ever spoken to Alice. Her words seemed to come far easier now, with more clarity and with much more emotion than she had shown with Alice. This, Alice realized, was her native tongue, and she knew there was something to be respected happening here. On the other hand, it was most rude to speak in a manner that not everyone understood. Not to mention the etiquette!

"You could at least greet a guest!" she snapped at them both. "And speak in a manner that can be understood by all parties! I daresay, I've never—"

"Please wait, Alice of Wonderland," Tiger Lily told her, though her father ignored Alice completely. "I am asking all of our questions. Perhaps wait over there. A seat will be nice."

Alice let out a huff and went to the side. She thought she had never been so poorly treated before, though she was fairly certain that was not true. There were people here, she noted, men and women but very few children or people her own age. They had selected their people to come back, and they were people who were already battle weary and all very tired. They looked at Alice with distrust, not wanting anything to do with her or with the task that they could now hear Tiger Lily speaking about. She heard some words echo in other voices around her, but no one would translate for her.

This was boring. Alice wandered the edge of the small encampment until she spotted something moving out in the forest. It was a strange thing to see, she thought. With so many people here, even in the distance of the darkness there should be nothing, but this thing was holding a small light, possibly a fire. It was a curious thing, but her hands were a bit cold and perhaps she could share in some of the fire. The warmth might do something to help warm these cold people and let them find a way to actually speak to her. It was outrageous that they were not doing even that much for her right now.

She took three steps through the woods to find that the fire was moving away. It seemed silly to have a fire moving *away* from people. She still followed it out until she finally realized this was quite a silly thing. She knew how to get close enough to it, and she would not be led around on a chase any longer.

Alice reached out and grabbed the torch. It went suddenly still as she pulled it out of the hand and brought it to herself. It was delightfully warm, and she enjoyed the light around her and in her hands. She was quite pleased with herself. With it in hand, she started to walk casually back through the woods to the village. Tiger Lily, rude as she was, would be very cross with her if she found that Alice had wandered off.

Not that she meant to. There was something strange about what she was doing, though she wasn't sure what it was just yet. It would come to her. Soon, she would know what she was doing that was so strange. Until then, at least she had a flame to keep herself company. A flame in the dark woods. Filled with something. Something that she didn't like.

Something came crashing through the woods after her. She looked on as that something came toward her, something with only a few limbs who appeared very cross for no good reason. She didn't know what he wanted, but he was dressed *terribly* and she wanted no part of his company. He lunged at her.

Alice stepped away, appearing behind him and feeling quite cross with him. "Now, if you want something, you *ask for* it!" she snapped at him. "And if you really expect a positive response, you should try bathing more regularly. You smell very much like you may have forgotten to bathe for several years, if you don't mind my saying so."

The man in the terrible clothing turned and lunged at her once more. Alice was very displeased with what was happening and went around him to continue giving him a piece of her mind, not bothering to keep her voice down as she spoke or to keep the light from waving around as she continued to speak. "This is very rude! I don't know how your mother raised you, but I ought to have a word with her and tell her of your indiscretions! It is very impolite to grab a lady, let me tell you!"

"Alice?" came a voice from the ground behind her. There was a boy who stopped to stare at her, trying to make sense of what he was seeing. Once he was sure of it, he laughed. "Alice! That's not how you deal with a zombie! You— Oh crap!"

Alice blinked and then stared, waving the fire closer to see who was standing there. It looked like it might have been Lance, but younger. His hair was long like Adam's, but his voice was higher than either of them. He was a younger version of the two of them. One that had a sword in his hand that he was gladly brandishing and using to cut off limbs of the zombie that dove for Alice's fire.

"Matt!" Alice cried, pleased to see him, and then not pleased at all. No wonder it had taken so long to find him. He looked much younger than before. "Do you know how I've been looking for you?" she demanded, going to his side and ignoring the zombies that continued to appear out of the woods to come after them. He swung wide and she ducked, letting his blade catch someone before she popped back up and continued to be cross with him. "That was not very polite!" she snapped at him. "I am trying to— Would you leave us?" she demanded of one zombie. "Can't you see I am *trying* to have a conversation?"

"Alice, what are you doing?" Matt demanded, now growing worried as he started to fight back against them. He was having fun trying to cut them down, though clearly a little concerned that Alice didn't seem to be doing anything to defend herself. "Come on! Grab a sword and jump in! Just go for the head!"

"Now, I don't think that's very nice!" she told him. "Really, where have your manners gone?"

"Adam!" Tiger Lily yelled at the two of them. "Stop her! She's not well!"

"Oh, not her again," Matt muttered, though Alice was much more distracting. She was at his side and grabbed him by the ear, yanking him down. "Ow! Hey! We're fighting zombies!" He swung his sword out to get one of them, but Alice pulled him back down again.

"Now you listen. I have been looking for you for *ages* and it has *not been easy!* You need to learn to come when you are called! I have been informed it is very dangerous out here!"

"*More dangerous with you holding onto me!*" Matt snapped back at her, pulling himself free and going back after another zombie as Tiger Lily got closer. "Come on, you're making zombie fighting annoying! At least set something on fire!"

"I will have you know... I'm really tired."

The weariness hit her all at once and she felt herself falling asleep. Something caught her before she hit the ground and she was surrounded by the pungent scent of decay and flames. Around her, the shadows of the attackers got heavier, but Matt was already gone, taking off and leaving her on her own.

CHAPTER 19

The Pendragon

IT WAS OFFICIAL. Alice absolutely detested waking up in Neverland. Nothing good ever seemed to come of it. First, she woke up in a hole with an injured leg that took weeks to recover from. And now she woke up with a headache and none of the comforts of the hole. It was a hard surface that she was stuck on, and it was still cold. This was not better than a hole by any means.

Worse, she could feel something biting into her wrists and ankles stretched above and below, drawing her across the hard surface and holding her there. She couldn't even hold her head or rub her temples as they throbbed against her skull. There would be no vanishing her way in and out of them given how deep they seemed to cut into her. Whoever had put her in this did not wanted her moving, and Alice was not pleased about it.

She let out a groan as she let her eyes drift open to look around her. It was a room, but a strange one given how the ceiling looked like it was alive. It was like the underside of a tree but cold like the inside of a fridge, which was a strange combination of things to be. The room was well lit regardless, sun streaming in from somewhere that she couldn't see, and there were small lamps kept around the room to illuminate any corners. There were people standing around and not moving. They smelled of decay, like much of the room did, but she was already growing used to the scent. Something about that was deeply unsettling. More than that, she noticed nothing moved around her, but she was not alone.

Alice could see something out of the corner of her eye, a figure that had been there the whole time she was coming around. She let her head drop to the side and she jumped at the eyes staring directly at her. Another yelp escaped her, this time of pain as the restraints bit into her skin.

The boy wasn't impressed. He was tied so closely to her that she could feel his soft breath on her cheek. His brown eyes looked back into hers, and narrowed at the sight of her. The mop of blond hair on his head was damp with sweat and matted down as he wrinkled his nose and inspected her.

He didn't appear to be dangerous. Alice arched her neck back and around to see that he was also shackled down and unable to move from the table like she was. He didn't look like he was dead, even if he did smell. She looked back to him, finding that he didn't look any more impressed with her than the last time they had met eyes.

"Oh good," he said, his voice a hoarse whisper. "You're still alive." He didn't sound happy about it. "I guess it's still my turn."

Alice tugged again at the chains. She knew ways to get out of shackles, but she couldn't just send her hands away this time. She couldn't even feel her hands, the restraints much too tight on her wrists. It was like they were made for small children, much smaller than Alice.

"Not yet," she said. She didn't like her odds right now. Alice had already accepted not coming out was a possibility when she went into Neverland. One by one, she went through the list of things she had to do before she was gone, taking some solace in knowing that Tiger Lily knew enough to at least teach someone else to return hearts if she couldn't do it herself. And she'd at least seen Matt, hadn't she? Tiger Lily might have gotten him out, even if Alice was stuck here.

But Adrianna would remain asleep.

Any attempts to struggle free were futile and only hurt her wrists and legs the more she tried. She needed to think of something. Maybe a way so that she could cross that barrier without first becoming so... Wonderland as soon as she made her way over. That was what had happened, she knew, and it was the thing that was going to get her killed now.

"Where are we?" she asked, hoping that this boy had some sense about him. He was relaxed next to her and she wondered just how long he had been there. If he knew where Wendy and the black book was. If either of those things even mattered if she couldn't get herself free.

He let out a breath and thought about it. "Not really sure," he said. "There's a girl. You'll meet her soon. She comes in and she cuts people up, taking parts out of some and putting them in other people. Right now she's looking for someone smaller than me so she can take a *squishy bit*." He rolled his eyes at that, anger and frustration flooding his expression.

"I don't think that's how that works," Alice said, but she knew already that it was a futile thing to talk about. Even he let out a small laugh at her words. "So you're not a zombie because you aren't the right size?"

"I'm *parts*," he said bitterly. "The witch already took my hand. I should consider myself lucky she didn't take my head too, but she had a spare last time." He looked at her again, disdain clear in his narrowed eyes. "She might let you go, though. I don't think I've seen any women besides her since I've been here. Unless she would rather have your eyes than her own."

He stared at her for what felt like too long before he

relaxed against the table, looking up at the ceiling, and let out a breath. "I just wish whoever it was that kept cutting off their limbs would stop. It's not pleasant not knowing whether or not I'm going to be used for parts."

So that's what was going to finally finish her. Not the black book or the Queen of Hearts or the Bandersnatch, but going Wonderland in Neverland and getting herself harvested, taken apart piece by piece and put into other people. She gave one last futile attempt to pull herself free, but still the chains wouldn't move.

"Oh, you don't need to worry," he told her. "Wendy only brings boys in here to fix up. It would be unnatural having one of them running around with your head."

Alice stopped at that, blinking up at the ceiling before letting her face flop once more to the side and looked at him with wide eyes. "Wendy?" she asked. "This is where Wendy is?"

"Yeah," he said, trying to inch away from Alice's stare. "Why?"

"I was looking for her," Alice said, suddenly with a renewed desire to not get murdered here. "Wendy and the black book. There's something I need to find to save a friend of mine."

"Well, you're not saving anyone now," he told her. "Might as well get comfortable. There's going to be a lot of screaming in a bit. Hopefully from you."

Alice tugged at the chains again, but her wrists were burning now and she could feel something dripping off of them. There was a chance now, and she was about to find what she needed.

"Hey, you keep doing that and she'll come back!" he snapped at her. "What's your name, anyway? If she does use you for parts, the least I can do is try to remember your name until she finally takes my head too."

"Alice," she told him. There had to be some way out of this. She was so close, and all she needed to do now was find this Pendragon thing and she could get out of there. "Liddell."

"Arthur Pendragon," he said. "You might live long enough to tell someone about me."

Alice went very still next to him. He shifted again, but he couldn't move away any more than she could. This was what she was supposed to find. A who and not a what. She hoped she wasn't too late, that she could still get him free and that he would still work with a missing hand. Hopefully that wasn't what he needed to cure people.

"You're what he sent me to find," she said. "You're going to be able to save Adrianna."

He smiled, though it was patronizing. "I'm going to save another fair young maiden. Joy. I need to save *myself* first, I think, Alice. I don't suppose you have any ideas? My last one worked so well that she still took my hand."

She tried to think. She needed something. There had to be something she could do, something simple that she was overlooking. She was too close now to fail. She couldn't pull herself free and, even if she could, she didn't know how to undo the shackles. She didn't know where she was or how to even get out of here once they were free. But that couldn't stop her.

Think. She just had to...

Right. She was wearing Adam's coat. And in the pocket...

Alice tried to make her hands move. She couldn't feel them except when she forced them to do something, sending pins and needles through them. She held in a hiss of pain and tried to reach, to send them into her pocket, but she couldn't grab anything. She wasn't even sure if they were going in, or if the pain was just from moving them.

This wasn't working. "Can you reach into my pocket?" she asked Arthur. "I think I can get you out."

Arthur looked at her, trying to decide if he should mention that he was currently also attached to the table. He decided he would leave it for now and let out a sigh. "Which one?" he asked, resigning himself to what he needed to do.

"There's a fan in my right pocket, the one on my hip," she told him. "I just need to get my hands on that and I can get you out."

"How do you think a fan is going to—"

The footsteps were neither particularly loud or soft, but the creak of the wood was enough to make Arthur stop cold. His eyes were wide and staring at one part of the room, anxiously waiting for something to come. Alice wasn't sure what to expect, only that they might have to act fast. She didn't know who Wendy was, but from the stories, she knew not to take her lightly.

"Just help me get it out," Alice hissed at him before the steps got too close. She ignored the look she knew he was giving her and turned to the small entrance where the footsteps were coming from.

Chapter 20

Wendy

A GIRL WALKED down the wooden steps and into the large room. Her long black hair hung loose over her shoulders, caked at the end in uncomfortable clumps. Her skin was pale and sunken, like she hadn't eaten very much at all for a long time. She didn't appear bothered by it, though she did appear frail. She didn't step particularly heavily, walking over to inspect the specimens that she had been brought.

"A bit big," she said, her voice stronger than her body looked. She prodded at Alice, her fingers jabbing into her sides and a curious look crossing her face. She hopped on the table and knelt down next to Alice, ignoring her attempts to wriggle away as she poked and squeezed at her body. "Much too big and too small," she said quietly. "But where did they find a girl?"

"What are you doing?" Alice asked. Moving away was

futile, but at least she was almost done. Finally, the girl climbed off of her and back to the ground, still looking Alice over.

"I don't have much use for girls," she said. Her eyes shifted to look Alice in the face Alice saw her eyes staring back at her, black as her hair. This was definitely Wendy, and she could see why Peter was hesitant to come back. "Did Peter bring you? You aren't like the Indians. Or the mermaids. But the mermaids are all women, and the Indian girls are all very young or very old. Except the one. She has grown just enough to be of no more use to me."

"No," Alice told her. She didn't try to turn her head or look away as Wendy continued to inspect her stroking her arm and poking at it before running her fingers through her hair. On her other side, she heard Arthur hold in a sound of pain and knew she had to keep her distracted. "Peter didn't want to come back."

"He fears me now," she said. She wasn't speaking to Alice, her hands gliding over her to inspect her, to poke and prod and decide what she was dealing with. Finally, she looked away and her eyes went to the people standing around the room, looking between a few of them one by one. "He brought me here, you know. Brought many of us here. We couldn't leave until he was bored of us, and then he would kill us. Or he said it was death. We knew it wasn't. He was too much of a coward for that."

"Was he?" Alice asked. Beside her, she could Arthur doing something to her pocket. He kept hitting her lightly, trying to get her attention. "What did he do instead?"

Alice looked back at Arthur, seeing the urgency on his face. His lips moved slow and forceful. *Now what?*

Hand, Alice mouthed back. She looked upward at her own hand and saw something strange. Arthur's arm wasn't up there any longer. She didn't keep looking long enough to figure out what happened to it, hearing Wendy let out a sigh and continue.

"He let them go," she said. "But he would never let me go. He never would have. He liked having a mother who would cook and clean and mend things for him. And so long as I was useful, I couldn't go anywhere. And my brothers, they liked it here too much. They never wanted to leave. And so I stayed. But it's not so bad now."

Alice heard the fan skidding next to her and felt Arthur moving. "It smells a little," she said, trying to keep her talking.

"You're not like them," Wendy told her, moving away to the side and to a closet. She opened it and it looked like there were very large sewing supplies inside, all of them old and just a little too big. In the middle was a black book propped open. Alice didn't much like what she was seeing and kept her attention on Wendy. "You feel like a real girl."

"Oh?" Alice asked. She did not like the sound of that. "What do you mean?"

"You have parts inside you," she said. She started looking through the sewing materials, picking up a needle and shears experimentally before putting them back down again. She flipped open and through the book for a page and continued to ponder her instruments. "There are those from Neverland and those that have been brought in. Those from Neverland, they are missing many of their insides. I've opened them up and there's many empty spots. The Lost Boys, those not from Neverland, they have far more parts on the inside. I wonder if yours are the same. I haven't seen the inside of a girl before."

Alice wasn't sure what to make of any of that. "What do you mean?" she asked. She heard the fan skid past her head. It just needed to be in her hand. She hoped Arthur could do it.

"I don't know what they're called," Wendy said. "Organs? But there are more inside if you are real. People from Neverland, they're missing them. But it's so bloody inside them. All of the empty spots are just filled with blood. It makes it very messy to replace pieces, but easy to get the parts. But for the real ones, it makes them much more difficult to put back together."

Out of the corner of her eye, she thought she saw the fan lift off the table on its own. She bit her tongue to keep quiet.

Arthur looked like he was concentrating very hard, and she looked back over to make sure Wendy still wasn't looking.

"But if you can't find the parts, then why bother replacing them at all?" Alice asked. "Best to just start over with something a little simpler, maybe find something to substitute."

"I've tried substitutions," Wendy told her. "But both of you are much too large for the things I am missing right now. Poor Michael, he needs a squishy thing on his right. But you're much too large. I wonder what I should do with you two. So many parts that won't fit in anything else. But I wonder..."

Alice's eyes flew open as she clamped her mouth shut. A million tiny needles stabbed into her hand as the fan glided into it and she forced herself to hold onto it. She could feel her fingers now and they were not happy with her as she forced herself to spread the fan open. She really hoped this worked.

"You wonder?" she asked. She needed to keep her talking and distracted, though it seemed Wendy was doing that just fine on her own. Slowly, carefully, she waved the fan at Arthur and kept her attention on Wendy.

"I saw something about how to make a quilt," she told her. "I do wonder what would happen if... huh. Now you're much too small to do anything."

Alice looked over and saw Arthur, looking very confused about his new height. He sat up next to her, now barely three feet tall and looking very alarmed at Wendy gliding closer.

He jumped off the table and away, cradling his left arm in his hands and Alice saw what he was talking about before. His left hand was gone and his wrist had been torn up far more than his right. She glanced up at the shackles and saw the trail of blood going from one down to her pocket.

"Get him back here," Wendy said, more irritated than anything else. She snatched the fan from Alice's hand and looked at it, frowning and unable to figure out what it was. She tossed it aside, letting it skitter across the floor.

The zombies standing around the room, all in partial states of repair, moved quickly to snatch the scrambling Arthur before he could get too far. One man held him up, Arthur struggling in his hands and trying to fight free as he yelled.

"Let me go!" he demanded. His feet kicked helplessly as they dangled off the ground. "I command you to let me go! What did you do to me, Alice? This is useless!"

Wendy beckoned him over and he continued to kick and yell at them the whole way. He spat in her face and turned away, but she grabbed him by the chin and turned it back to face her. "If you can't keep that tongue still, I will remove it for you," she told him. "Although you are small enough now. Perhaps you have the squishy thing I need for Michael."

Arthur was screaming at her, but Wendy wasn't bothered. She pondered it for a moment before she nodded, satisfied with herself. "Maybe a little small, but that means the squishy thing will fit. Lock him down. I think I can take the squishy thing."

Arthur continued to yell profanities, but he was locked next to Alice again in moments. The shackles were adjusted to his new small stature and, though he tried, he could not get free. "Do you know who I am?" he demanded. "You can't do this to me! People will come for me! My knights will find me and they will make you pay!"

"No knights have ever come to Neverland," Wendy said calmly. She pinched his nose and poured something in his mouth. Arthur choked and tried to cough it out, but Wendy only gave him a pat. "Quiet and still, now. Can't have you moving around like last time."

Arthur went very quiet and still next to Alice. He said nothing, but his eyes were still open and moving. Wendy left for only a moment and returned with materials in hand. She was like a child ready to operate on him like he was a teddy bear, none of the seriousness of what was happening showing on her face. She picked up his shirt and started to cut it away.

"You don't have to do that," Alice said. She needed Arthur alive. She was pretty sure if Wendy took this squishy thing, he would not be alive anymore.

"Do you need to be quieted as well?" Wendy asked.

Alice shut up, blood running cold as Wendy took up the scissors and picked the place she was going to start cutting.

This was it. Adrianna's last hope was gone. It would only be a matter of time before Alice would also be cut up. She didn't even know if she was going to make it to tomorrow.

Wendy pondered and then moved the scissors to Arthur's midsection, open and intent to make the first cut. Alice looked away and closed her eyes, unable to watch. A scream pierced the air, but it wasn't Arthur's.

CHAPTER 21

Better Late

ALICE LOOKED SHARPLY over into the air where the scream came from, seeing the last of Peter as he disappeared through a hole in the ceiling between the roots of the trees. She wondered what he had been doing here and why he was here at all. But that was answered quickly in the company he left behind.

"More materials," Wendy said, almost casually before turning back to Arthur. "Grab them, would you, please?" she asked of her zombies.

She went back to trying to remember where the first cut would start. A knife came flying across the room, hitting the scissors out of her hand. She blinked down and looked, seeing that Adam had not only thrown it, but he already had another and he was tearing into one of her zombies. He went closer to Alice while Tiger Lily covered his back. Wendy looked less than impressed at what was going on.

Adam managed to cut and work his way close enough to Alice, looking very disappointed. "You had to get brought right to Wendy, didn't you?" he demanded of her, clearly not happy with what had happened but not able to bring himself to be too mad. Another of Wendy's minions came down the stairs, and it seemed that they couldn't quite get rid of them fast enough.

"Matt says you cut off the head," Alice offered.

He opened his mouth to say something, but shut it again. "Questions later," he said, striking his knife hard into the shackles around Alice's wrists and wrenching them apart. Alice pulled her hands free and Adam jumped around the table to get her feet free. Alice twitched her fingers, but pain shot through her hands still when she tried to move them. Her hands were the wrong color, pale and tinged with blue. Her feet didn't move at all inside her shoes.

Adam left, suddenly distracted by the swarm of undead bodies coming upon them. He worked through them with Tiger Lily as best he could, keeping them off and looking around for some reprieve. Next to her, Arthur was still attached to the table by shackles she couldn't hope to remove with her hands as they were and not moving.

Alice reached to the side and forced her hand to close

around the fan. She brought it back to her and fanned Arthur, letting him get small enough that he could be easily carried. Wincing, she dropped the fan and took a deep breath. Zombies all around them, and she could barely use a fan. She couldn't let her hands stop her now.

"Sorry," she told him, clumsily scooping him up and dropping him in one of the front pockets. She was not leaving without him, no matter how her body didn't want her to move. She took a deep breath and stared down at her hands, flexing her fingers and trying to rub the feeling back into them so she could feel something other than the pins and needles.

"Give me back my coat!" Adam snapped at her as he spun closer to her. Alice stared at him, but it was not a request. When she didn't hand it over, Adam yanked it off of her. "Careful! Arthur's in the pocket."

"Don't care," Adam told her. He shrugged it on between stabs and moved, light on his feet, as he danced around the table. He did have a stunning amount of accuracy, and she could see the movements he made mimicking Tiger Lily's at times, and the Mad Hatter's at others. He had learned from them both, and he was apparently a very good student. "We need to get out of here. Get off the table!"

Alice didn't so much hop off the table as she fell off of it. She didn't feel her feet land on the floor, but she did feel the rest of her smack against it and roll into a body that had fallen to Adam's side. She didn't see what Adam had done, only the look of irritation on his face as he reached back down with both hands and picked Alice up. When she couldn't balance, he sat her on the table and nodded at it.

There was now a large metal circle on the table. A mirror. Oh, so that was the plan. "Got it," she told him, trying to think of a good place to open the portal to Wonderland to and settling on the White Rabbit's house. "Get Tiger Lily."

Around them, the zombies had thinned out. Tiger Lily was easy to spot, but she wasn't alone.

Wendy had pinned Tiger Lily to the wall, held there by a few of her zombies. She looked Tiger Lily over, shoving her scissors deep into Tiger Lily's stomach, shaking her head. "No wonder Peter liked me more," she said. "You tried too hard to make him like you, but in the end he always came back to me. Because I'm real."

She twisted them in Tiger Lily's gut, but Tiger Lily didn't break eye contact with her. She wouldn't even wince.

"Would you like to be a real girl?" Wendy asked her. "I can do that for you now. I have the materials."

Adam was on Wendy like a madman, pulling her back by her long hair and throwing her down to the ground in one movement. He grabbed Tiger Lily with his other arm and pulled her back to the mirror and to Alice. "Go now!" he yelled at her.

"You first," Alice said, ushering the two of them closer. They dove into the mirror and Alice fell in after them, the mirror sealing shut before anything else might be able to slip through.

THE WHITE RABBIT did not appreciate when Tiger Lily fell into him, followed by two more bodies. Tiger Lily groaned in pain as Alice and Adam scrambled off of her, Adam saying nothing in greeting and heading right for one of the shelves in the White Rabbit's house. He pulled out a small kit that looked like he knew what to do with it.

"I am fine," Tiger Lily snapped at him, taking the kit from him and starting to put herself back together. Adam tried to protest, but she pushed him off of her and started to stitch herself up, suddenly very unwilling to allow him to help her with a stab wound. Alice did note that she didn't seem nearly as injured as she should have been after getting stabbed.

"You got—"

"I am *fine*," she snapped at him, waving him away. "Leave me. See if she was successful and tell her she is not going back." Tiger Lily shot him one final glare before she continued to work on herself.

Adam wasn't happy when he bent down next to Alice. She sat with her hands in her lap, feet stretched out in front of her and trying to breathe. She didn't know what her face must have looked like to make Adam look away like that, or why he looked so apologetic when he looked back. She just wanted to forget that happened.

"Can you get up?" he asked.

Alice tried to speak, but her voice caught. She shook her head, looking at her feet. She reached for them but winced as she tried to move her hands.

Adam caught her by the arm and looked over her hands and wrists. His eyes went down to her ankles. "I'm going to take off your shoes," he told her. "You tell me what the hell is going on here."

Alice took a breath and looked at her hands again. They were returning to the right color, however slowly. "I found the Pendragon," she said. "It's the guy in your pocket. Arthur Pendragon. The Bandersnatch said that he could wake up Adrianna."

Adam got her shoes and socks off. Alice could feel the movement of the fabric coming off her feet as a dull pain that threatened to turn into pins and needles like her hands. They looked much more blue than her hands had. "Jesus Christ, Alice," he muttered. "It's a miracle you haven't gotten yourself killed already."

"You're not supposed to be here," Alice said absently.

"And you're not supposed to get captured by Wendy!"

Adam snapped back at her. "You're *lucky* I got back when I did!"

Alice shrank back, staring at her hands again. They didn't hurt as much when she moved them now, at least. "We should put him back," she said, not looking back from her hands. "Finding him was the whole point."

Adam stayed there for only a moment longer before he backed away. He fished in his pockets until he pulled out Arthur and put him on the table. He fished a vial of something out of another pocket and uncorked it. Gently, he poured a drop of it in Arthur's mouth and pocketed it again.

It wasn't a fast process or a slow one, but it was even. Arthur regrew on the table, expanding and stretching and scaling until he looked just a little too big to be normal. All at once at the end, he snapped back to size and sat bolt upright, eyes fixed on every person in the room one by one.

"What have you done to me?" he demanded of Alice. "I've had my *fill* of witches for several lifetimes! If those lifetimes could stop, that would also make me grateful." He got to his feet and loomed over Alice, much taller than she was expecting him to be. "What did you do to me?"

"She just shrunk you," Adam said, pulling him back from her. "Jesus Christ, what is your problem?"

Arthur pulled himself off of Adam, but Alice wasn't bothered. She looked up from her hands. "We need to get you to a hospital," she told him. "You don't have a hand. It looks like it's not healing well." He was still bleeding from where he'd pulled his wrist free and oozing from the stump. Alice thought it might be going green.

"*You* need a hospital," Adam insisted.

"It's not—"

"Take her back," Tiger Lily told them from across the room. Her injury looked patched now and it was no longer bleeding. "Adam, you will take them both back."

"You need me here," he insisted. "When she's gone—"

"This place is not your responsibility," she told him firmly. "Alice of Wonderland needs to return and you will take her back. And remove *him*." She glared at Arthur, but said nothing more about him. Alice was certain she was trying to warn Alice about something with her look, but Alice had no idea what.

"Fine," Adam said tightly. "Both of you need a hospital."

"I have no interest in whatever the witch wants for me," Arthur said.

"There's no *witches* in a hospital," Adam told him, exasperated. "They're just going to fix that thing that used to be a hand. You can't really expect me to believe that he's going to save Addie," he said to Alice, demanding some kind of answer.

"That's what's supposed to happen," she told him. Behind him, the mirror reflected her the washroom at the hospital. She let out a breath and looked back at Tiger Lily. "I'm sorry, I…"

"You will return one day, Alice of Wonderland," Tiger Lily told her firmly. "You must find someone else who can return the hearts. But I will watch your books. And do as you ask."

"Thank you," Alice said. "And I'll be back. Soon. I promise."

Adam wasn't happy as he picked Alice up, but he did it anyway. He beckoned Arthur over with a nod, indicating the mirror and the white room lined with stalls on the other side. "Come on," he told Arthur, pushing him through the mirror first. "You get to learn what a hospital is."

CHAPTER 22

Bedside Manner

THREE KIDS COMING to the desk of long term care from the washroom was strange enough, saying nothing of how they were dressed. That one of them was being carried and another was missing a hand sent them into action and the nurses descended on them.

Arthur was the larger curiosity out of them. They took him away to tend to the stump of an arm, Arthur looking more irritated by their concern than anything else. Still he allowed them to look it over and take him away to properly tend to it. Somehow, they didn't ask nearly as many questions of him.

The doctor told Alice she would recover, even if he wasn't happy about her silence about the source of any of this. Somehow, Adam had managed to get her mother on the phone who gave them whatever information they needed. She was given something to keep her calm so her circulation could fix itself and left to rest with Adam while the feeling slowly came back to her feet and hands.

Adam hung up with his family and sat back in the chair next to Alice, frowning and looking off into the corner of the room. They sat in silence for far too long before he spoke. "I don't like him. This is weird."

"A lot of stuff is weird," Alice told him. She moved her foot and winced as the tingling turned sharp. Standing wouldn't be fun. "But he's going to get Adrianna to wake up."

Adam was silent at that and she could see him working to find the holes in it. He shook his head and looked back down at his phone, fingers moving over it as he continued to message home.

"Thank you," she said finally. "For coming back."

"I'm staying next time," he told her.

"Peter brought you?" It seemed obvious to her now, knowing that she had seen him in a brief flash before he had flown off and away.

"Tiger Lily got in touch," he said. "Said she needed help. Said you were in trouble. It was tricky getting hold of him, but she said he could get me and he did."

"You're going to try to make him take you back again."

"Not until I know what the deal is with that guy you found."

"Arthur is going to save Adrianna."

"You keep saying that." He didn't believe it, but he watched as Alice winced again and stayed quiet. "You're lucky you're getting off so easy. Any longer and they might have had to cut them off. How long were you there for?"

Alice shrugged. "I was unconscious."

"Your feet were blue. It had to have been hours." He let out a deep, beleaguered sigh. "You don't go into Neverland, Alice. That's why it's called *Never*land."

The door opened and Arthur came in, stump of an arm freshly bandaged. Unlike Alice, he only had bruising around his ankles and wrists. A doctor walked in with him, eyes glazed over as he guided him to the other bed.

"Why is he being put in here?" Adam asked, eyeing them.

"If you and the witch insist on bringing me here to rescue some maiden, then you can deal with this," he said, waving at the doctor. "He keeps asking things."

"I really don't like him," Adam muttered darkly.

The doctor took a seat next to Arthur and looked down at his clipboard. "And what did you say your name was?" he asked.

"Ask them," Arthur said, nodding to Alice. "She'll be able to answer everything."

"I think it's better if I ask you, as you're the patient."

"I *said* to—"

"This isn't your room," the doctor added, alarmed and looking back at Alice and Adam. "We shouldn't be in here."

Irritation spread across Arthur's face. He made an attempt at a gesture, but the stump of a left hand did not do what he needed it to. He tried to do something else with his right and the doctor's eyes went very wide. And then he was gone, replaced with a very large lizard.

"Shrink him," Arthur commanded Alice. "You're good at that, at least."

Alice's eyes grew wide in amazement. "How did you do that?"

Adam was on his feet and three steps closer to the door. "*Put him back.*"

"He'll change back on his own," Arthur said, looking much more annoyed than anything else as the large lizard started to wander the room, pondering its new existence.

Adam looked back to Alice, but she only shrugged. "He's your problem," Adam told her sharply. He left, letting the door slam shut behind him.

The large lizard wasn't dangerous. It was already showing signs of becoming human again. Alice wasn't sure what Adam was so concerned about, though her mind was still spinning from whatever they had given her to help her recover.

She reached and she could feel the tingle her fingers now emitted when she grabbed the clipboard. It was less painful now, at least, but she still didn't feel like holding things. She brought it back to look over the notes on the clipboard. There was little about his condition on here, Alice not recognizing any of the medical jargon that was written down. The sheet on top was an intake form, one looking for his basic information.

Experimentally, she picked up the attached pen, but her fingers wouldn't curl around it properly. Frowning, she let it go and let the board rest on her lap. "I can't fill this out for you," she said.

"Where have you taken me?" he demanded.

"Washington," Alice said. "Out of Neverland."

"And that house with the people. The ones with the holes in their chests."

"That was Wonderland," Alice told him. "Where are you from?"

"Camelot," he said.

"So, like, Rhode Island?"

"I don't know what you're talking about," he told her. "Will they return my hand?"

"They might be able to reattach it if they have it," Alice suggested. She watched as the lizard continued to shift back into a human man. "They're going to need your name," she told him.

"They don't respect the name Pendragon here as they should."

"You could use Penn," she suggested.

It looked like Arthur was trying to decide who was dumber, Alice or the lizard man now curled up against the door. Alice didn't know what he decided when he let out a tired sigh. "You keep saying I'm going to save this Adrianna," he told her. "Why?"

"The Bandersnatch said you would," she told him. "She was put to sleep and now she won't wake up."

"And why should I?" he asked. "You've done nothing for me. You shrunk me down, shoved me into a pocket, and brought me here where they've done nothing but poke and prod at me and tell me that I am never getting my hand back."

"I'm sorry," Alice told him. "What happened to your hand?"

"It got cut off!" he snapped at her, waving the stump at her. "Cut off by that witch using one of his books!"

"Whose books?"

"Merlin's!"

Alice didn't know who that was and she didn't care about asking any further. She was more curious about why, but she didn't want to make him mad. She needed him to agree.

"Please," she implored him. "She's sick and I was told you could save her."

"I'll be doing nothing to help witches," he told her firmly. "They've done nothing but make my life a misery. Cut off my hands, plunge my home into turmoil, whatever they want."

"Adrianna's not a witch," Alice said. "She has nothing to do with any of this. Someone tried to curse me with it, but they got her instead. She didn't do anything to deserve it. She's normal."

"And what are you?"

"Not a problem," she told him. "In fact, in a couple months I'll be gone forever."

Arthur looked at that, curious. "The Bandersnatch," he said, quiet as he looked Alice over. A moment passed and his eyes widened. "Oh you stupid girl. You're no real witch at all, are you?"

"I never said I was."

"But he was still willing to make a deal." Something about that was interesting to him and he pondered it, eyes drifting over her. They lingered on the bandages around her wrists, then down to her ankles, then back to his own stump of a hand. "Take me to this friend of yours."

"I don't think I can walk yet."

Arthur let out a deep sigh and got out of bed. "Perhaps you should try to not be so small that she needed to use the child shackles on you." Still, he scooped Alice up nudged the lizard doctor out of the way, and they made their way through the hospital.

Despite how strangely Arthur was dressed — and he was dressed very strangely — no one paid him any attention and let him go about his business as he pleased, letting him walk past without so much as a second glance as they went through the halls to long term care. Adrianna's room was down the hall and no one stopped them until they entered the room.

Adam was on his feet, shoulders rising as soon as he saw who was on the other side. He stood in the way and wouldn't let them in. His eyes flickered down to Alice, not happy that she was out of bed, then to Arthur who he was just not happy to see at all.

Arthur looked him over for only a moment, wrinkling his nose at the coat he wore before shoving Alice into his arms. "Here," he said. "Take her."

Adam fumbled and his phone clattered to the ground, but he got Alice easily in his arms and growled after Arthur as he walked past them. "You shouldn't even be out of bed," he told her as he put her down across the chairs. She kept the discomfort to herself when he propped her feet up on an arm rest. "You know you were tricked, right? That thing sent you to Neverland for no reason."

"I had to," Alice told him. "I needed to get—"

"You know how dangerous it is there!" he told her. "The Bandersnatch obviously lied to you to get you out of the way early. He probably wants out of this bet now because you're doing nothing to save yourself!"

"It's fine," Alice told him. "Tiger Lily knows how to put the hearts back—"

"But she can't actually do it!" Adam told her.

"She can teach someone," Alice said. She could see Adam growing redder, but she wasn't sure why. Perhaps she was too calm about it, but she couldn't bring herself to get worked up.

"No, *you* are going to keep putting those hearts back. We can't just *hope* Tiger Lily can teach someone else. You're getting way too reckless, Alice. Life doesn't just move on when you go."

"Actually it will," Alice reminded him. "Evan went and no one even noticed he was gone. Sarah too. And you guys don't even know who Wyatt is, and Adrianna was dating him. So it'll be fine when I go."

"I think we'll notice if you die first, Alice."

"That's probably the same for you," she told them. "I can't even stop you from going back to Wonderland now, can I? Peter can drop you off in Neverland. You can ask Tiger Lily to show you how to get to Wonderland from there. She might even be able to show you how to return the hearts. I probably shouldn't have spent so much time trying to get you back if Peter was just going to put you back you anyway."

"Not the point, Alice!"

"Oh, but Matt's in Neverland," she told him. "He was telling me how to fight zombies. Since you have a way back, then maybe you can—"

"Don't change the subj— Hey!"

Alice's eyes followed Adam's to Adrianna's bed. Arthur had decided now was the best moment to kiss her unconscious friend, in a moment when neither of them was paying attention.

Alice was forgotten in an instant. Adam stormed over to Arthur with far too much speed for how heavy that coat was and he ripped him off. Arthur had barely hit the ground when Adam was on him, landing a blow directly to his jaw and following up with another to his face.

Arthur's cries of pain were enough to bring a nurse running and security soon followed. Alice stayed very still spread across the chairs, eyes open only a crack to watch as they broke up the fight. Adam went quietly, tossing his coat over Alice as he left, while Arthur was escorted out by a nurse already looking at his bloody nose.

Once the door closed and she was alone, Alice wiggled out from under the coat, a hiss escaping her. It hurt when it landed on her, but at least she had it back. She took Adam's coat with both hands and placed it back in her dorm room to deal with later. If he was going to try to go back again, she wanted to make it difficult.

Alice got gingerly to her feet, her legs screaming for her to put them back up. She wobbled and every step felt like walking on a bed of needles, but she forced herself to keep going step by step. Arthur was supposed to help Adrianna. That didn't look like he was helping.

As she got closer, Adrianna moved. It was only a little at first, her head falling to one side, but it was more than Alice had seen. She wobbled closer, watching her intently until she saw her eyes crack open.

"Alice?" Adrianna asked, her voice parched as she looked around at the machines hooked up to her and wondering what was going on. "Where am I?"

CHAPTER 23

The New Adrianna

ALICE WAS HAPPY to take the afternoon off. Her choice of long sleeves in the warm late spring weather was causing a few people to eye her carefully. There was also some of the talk about the strange one-handed boy found on campus that Adam was quick to claim credit for finding.

And, of course, Heather was mad at her for ditching her before the break properly began. Alice couldn't blame her. She hadn't expected to come back from spring break at all, and she almost wished she hadn't. But at least Adrianna was awake and released from the hospital.

"Alice!" Adrianna said, grabbing her in a hug and squeezing her tight. "Sorry I didn't stay in touch. They didn't let me keep my phone. They wanted to run so many tests to make sure I was okay." She pulled back and looked at Alice. "Are you okay? You didn't look okay. Did you lose weight?"

She was just happy Adrianna was back. Alice hadn't even spent a day in the hospital and they only made a passing mention that she'd gotten out of her room and into Adrianna's. Adrianna had looked so confused when she woke up, not sure how much time had passed or why she wasn't in the dorms. She was worried she'd missed handing in her assignment and it had taken a few minutes to explain that wasn't a problem anymore.

"I'm so sorry," Alice said. "I didn't know it was poison."

"The danish?" she asked. "It's fine. It's not like I knew either." She smiled and hugged Alice once more before sitting her down on the bed. "I thought Lori gave you those. I don't think she's someone who we should be worried about poisoning you, though. It seems like a strange thing to do for her."

Alice shook her head. "It was Claudia," she said. "Your stepmom. She's kind of mad that I took her book from her and she made them, I think. I don't know what she did, but Peter told me that was what happened. At least, he told me the apple one was... What are you doing?"

Adrianna had her hand on Alice's forehead, tipping her chin up and looking at her in the eyes. "Your eyes are a little milky," she said. "Did you do something?"

Alice shrugged and pulled away. "Heather's a little mad at me right now," she told her, looking off to the side. "I kind of ditched her to go to Wonderland and get Arthur to wake you up."

Adrianna smiled, though her eyes went down at Alice's wrists peeking out from under her sleeves. She let Adrianna take the bandages off, letting the cuts and marble of bruises get some air. Adrianna bit her tongue again, stopping herself from whatever it was she was about to say. "You know, that's about the right spot for a watch," she told Alice. "Or a bracelet. You should know better."

Alice blinked. There was something strange about her and she knew it, but she wasn't sure what. Maybe it was the number of questions. Or it was the fact that she kept noticing things Alice would rather she didn't. Still, Adrianna got up and went to her drawer before the washroom. She came back with a few bracelets to cover some of Alice's wrists and the salve and gauze to rewrap her injuries. "You need to take better care of yourself."

"It's okay," Alice said. "It doesn't really hurt."

"Not really the point," Adrianna told her. "Just because I've been sleeping for months doesn't mean that you get to go getting yourself in trouble, Alice. Lance and Adam have told me some stuff about what's been going on. You said Wendy was dangerous."

"And now I know how dangerous," Alice told her. "It's fine. I'm not going back there anymore."

"And the Bandersnatch?"

"Dealt with."

Adrianna stopped and let out a sigh. She continued to work Alice's wrists with the salve and gently wrapped them back up. "Alice, you haven't," she told her. "I know you haven't. They told me you haven't."

"It's fine. I figured something out."

Alice could tell Adrianna didn't believe her and it was unsettling. She'd never not believed her before. The look was new, the look of considering the best way to break it to her that she knew she was lying and how to get her to be honest, it was something Alice didn't like.

A knock at the door interrupted them. "Come in," Alice said, grateful for the reprieve.

Miss Amanda opened the door with a smile. "Hello Adrianna," she said brightly. Standing just behind her, Adam peered into the room and gave them a wave. "You good for a visitor?"

"Adam!" Adrianna said, jumping to her feet. She went to hug her brother, laughing and chiding him for taking so long. The siblings hugged and launched into chatter, Adrianna showing him in while Miss Amanda slipped in to have a word with Alice.

"You've been missing counseling appointments," she told her quietly.

"Adrianna is back," Alice said. "There's no reason to keep going now, right?"

"We're worried about you, Alice. You were getting better when you were going to them."

"I..." she started, but she was distracted. Out of the corner of her eye, she saw someone moving. A blond boy with brown eyes and one hand staring back at her, watching her. She turned to look, but he wasn't anywhere in sight. Frowning, she turned back to Miss Amanda. "What happened to Arthur?" she asked. "The boy with the missing hand."

"More like taken," a voice muttered in the air. She twitched to see where it was coming from, and she noticed both Adrianna and Adam did as well.

"We've been trying to find his family," Miss Amanda said patiently. She knew Alice was trying to steer the conversation away and very carefully considered her next words. "Dr. Aliya is currently keeping an eye on him. If you know anything about where he came from..."

"Will I get in trouble for not going anymore?" Alice asked. Again, out of the corner of her eye, she could see Arthur watching her.

"No, but—"

"Walk?" Adrianna asked loudly. "Sorry, Miss Amanda. Um, can we take Alice with us?"

Miss Amanda smiled. "Sure," she said. "We'll talk more later."

Alice nodded and got her shoes. She was grateful to be getting out of there and into the sunshine, even if she could feel a pair of eyes on her back the whole time. At first, she thought it was just Miss Amanda being far too concerned about her, but they seemed to follow as they continued walking.

She was only barely listening as Adam and Adrianna talked, Adrianna asking for more details about when he'd gotten back and marvelling at how they had all thought it was fine that he was gone. She didn't understand how he was still so calm about Matt being missing, especially when he now knew that he was in Neverland and how terrible Wendy was.

Alice's attention was on her surroundings. She could see Arthur following her out of the corner of her eye, only to be gone when she tried to look at him. She was almost sure he was saying something, but she couldn't quite make out anything he wanted with the soft breeze dragging his words just a little too far away to hear. She forced herself to keep walking, to breathe normally and to try and look more quickly to catch him, but he was never there.

Adam slipped in next to her and rested a hand on her shoulder. "Don't look directly at him for a minute," he said.

Alice inhaled a short breath and looked wide eyed back at Adam and Adrianna. They both nodded, Adrianna smiling and hooking an arm around Alice's shoulders. "I think he moves every time you look," she said, her head leaned in close to Alice's and keeping her walking as Adam went off the path. "Who is he? Adam just gets mad when I ask."

"He woke you up," Alice said. "His name's Arthur Pendragon. I found him in Neverland."

"Is he *from* Neverland?"

Alice shrugged. "I don't know much about Neverland. Just that it hurts a lot more than Wonderland." Her fingers trailed down to her wrists again, lightly brushing the bruising. Parts of her feet still felt funny.

Adrianna squeezed her shoulders tighter. "You don't have to go back."

"I probably should," she said. "I found Matt. I should get him back too."

"You're staying right here with me," Adrianna insisted. She kept Alice there for a moment longer before she let out a small laugh and let go of her shoulder. "And it looks like Adam got him. You want to see what he wants?"

She took Alice by the hand and tugged her to where Adam was now kneeling. Under him, Arthur didn't look quite right. He wasn't quite there, though Alice couldn't place why. She couldn't see through him like the ghosts in the movies, but there was also something about him that was just not present. Adam looked like he was only barely holding him in place.

"This is ridiculous," Arthur said. Adam lurched to the ground as Arthur disappeared from under him and appeared standing.

"You're following us," Adrianna said. "Why?"

"Because she said some very interesting things the last time we met that I want to know more about," he told them. "Things I assume she wouldn't want her friends to know about. I was trying to do her a favour and give her the option of coming to talk on her own. Unfortunately, it seems her friends are nosy."

"Disappearing every time she looked was supposed to help?"

"You seem to think I'm actually here."

"What do you want, Arthur?" Alice asked.

"Some idiot has released the Bandersnatch," he said. "We have... shall we say, some history. It took a very long time to lock him up last time and it looks like I'm going to need to do it again. I want to know how many deals he's made. I know there's at least one bet," he added, eyeing Alice, "but if he hasn't made too many then he might not be an immediate concern."

"What's the difference between a deal and a bet?" Adam asked. His eyes also strayed to Alice, but they shot back sharply to Arthur, ready to grab him again if he tried to get away.

"A deal is a trade," Arthur said. "Give him someone of

some importance and he will grant you whatever you desire. Make a bet and, well…" He smiled at Alice, staring at her and slowly leaning in closer as he spoke. "I do wonder what you wanted so badly that you decided to trade your life for it. And I hope you know you're never going to get it. He was never going to give it to you."

Alice stepped back and she was gone, appearing back alone in her dorm. She felt warm and kicked off her shoes before curling up next to her bed. Her breaths came deep and fast, none of the air ever feeling like it hit her lungs. She swiped at her wrists, Adrianna's bracelets clattering to the floor as she tried to keep breathing and block out everything.

There was no reason for this. She knew she was going. She had given up. She had a task and she failed to do it. Once the people she knew were out, she had stopped trying so hard and now it was too late to find a way out. She had made a bet and lost. Made a deal and not followed through on it. It was fair.

At least, she thought it was fair. That she had a chance.

Alice heard the door open and glanced under her arm to see Adrianna come in. Neither of them moved for a long moment. Finally, she heard Adrianna shuffle and felt an arm fall over her shoulders. Adrianna said nothing, sitting quietly with her as Alice kept trying to breathe.

CHAPTER 24

Pointless

ADRIANNA SETTLED BACK into the routine as best she could. Alice was surprised at how quickly she was able to pick up everything she had missed. She was permitted to take her midterms the next week so she could graduate with the rest of them and she passed them easily. She picked up the material much more quickly than she had before, encountering none of the stumbling blocks.

She was different now. Alice didn't know how to feel about that.

Still, Alice tried not to think about it. There wasn't much time left before the end of the year and she was just trying to spend as much time being happy as she could manage. It was hard with Arthur lingering in the corner of her vision at unexpected moments, but she did her best to ignore him. If he wanted to talk to her, he could come talk to her directly and tell her how stupid she was. It was too late to do anything about it now.

Heather refused to talk to her. She knew Alice had finally showed up after four days with Adam and some handless boy in the hospital just in time for Adrianna to wake up again, but she was pissed that Alice had ditched her for the week. The silence showed no sign of stopping, though it seemed no one was that surprised.

"Alice always disappears," Robert told her, not minding that Alice could hear him. "*Always.* None of this should surprise anyone anymore."

"Did I mention Peter ran off halfway through the break?" Kevin asked. "Dad wasn't worried *at all* for some reason, but he vanished about the same time Alice showed up again from the sounds of it."

"And then you showed up here with Alice," Heather said to Adam. Sarah glanced at Alice, as did Robert, but Heather wouldn't even look at her, instead glaring Adam down. "What the hell is going on?"

"You're reading too much into it," Adam told her, explaining the story for the hundredth time to her. "I came back to see Addie. Ran into Alice and her handless guy and helped them get to the hospital since I was heading that way anyway."

"This smells," Heather told him. "What are you hiding?"

"His hand," Adam said. "But don't tell him. We're trying to keep it a secret."

Heather stared at him. "Not funny."

"It's very funny."

She glared at him, shaking her head before getting back to work. "This whole thing stinks," she repeated. "You're all hiding something."

"You used to like my jokes."

"I liked it when you were *honest* with me."

Though she knew she deserved the cold shoulder from Heather, being so openly ignored was wearing on Alice. She just wanted to have a nice last couple months before she went, and Heather was making it very difficult to do that. For that matter, so was Adam. "Have you told her about Lily?" Alice asked.

Suddenly, Heather could hear her. Her eyes went wide and she turned slowly to look from Alice to Adam, not sure what it was she was supposed to think of that. Adam tensed, but brushed it off, looking as innocent and like he had done nothing wrong as possible. "I thought you didn't want me to talk about Lily," he said to Alice, the smile doing nothing to hide the fact that he was telling her to shut up.

"Who is Lily?" Heather asked, her voice slow and even and clearly letting Adam know he was in trouble.

"She's a friend," Adam said quickly. "A mutual friend."

"You've been missing for two years. You don't *have* mutual friends."

"She's more Alice's friend."

"Maybe you should *both* go hang out with her instead."

"Lily's busy," Alice told her absently. "Especially now."

"She could probably use a hand," Adam suggested.

"No."

"So…" Kevin said, looking uncomfortable. He stretched out the syllable and turned to Alice. "How did you find a guy with no hand wandering around?"

Alice shrugged. "I don't know. He didn't have it when I saw him."

"Where was he? Just wandering around?"

"Hey!" Adrianna called, making her way over to them. The mood changed almost immediately, Heather brightening up and backing off of Adam. As a group they relaxed, and Alice shrank away from the rest of them as the attention switched to Adrianna. It wouldn't have been so bad if everyone else hadn't been trying to help, but Adrianna was enough of a distraction to make them stop.

Out of the corner of her eye, she could see Arthur lingering there, watching. This time she turned to look at him and he didn't move away. Alice didn't know what he was looking at, but he didn't seem to be after her this time.

Alice considered pulling out homework, but pulled out her phone instead. She let them talk as she started up Robert's game and started to play quietly, matching colorful bricks together and passing the time until they broke apart and she felt like she could talk again.

Robert leaned into the middle of the group, waving a hand to get their attention. "Is that guy watching us?"

Sarah narrowed her eyes at the corner. "Yes he is," she told him, giving him a nod. Arthur made a sour face, his eyes going to Sarah and his right hand moving strangely. Sarah smiled at him before she looked back at Alice. "Is he this handless guy?"

"What are you talking about?" Kevin asked, looking in the same direction. "There's no one there."

Sarah went pale, but they were paying much more attention now. Adam watched Heather look, and the confusion over her face as she looked back at Sarah. "No one's there," she confirmed, though it was obvious that Adam disagreed.

"I'll be back," Adam said, getting up and going to the door. Alice let her eyes follow him, as did Kevin and Sarah's, as Adam went to the corner and hooked his arm in Arthur's as he passed, pulling him into the hall. Adrianna smiled at Alice, giving her arm a light squeeze.

"So movies tonight?" Adrianna suggested. "I feel like I've missed a lot."

Alice's phone buzzed. It was from Adam. *Outside. Now.*

With a sigh, Alice got to her feet and made her exit, leaving her things behind. Adrianna gave her a strange look as she went, but no one stopped her on her way out. The conversation continued like she had never been there at all.

Adam was alone when she went into the hall, lingering a little further down and waiting for her. She didn't see Arthur there, but she knew better than to assume she knew what Adam had done. He didn't have his coat and all of his things, but she didn't put it past him to have a few tricks still up his sleeves.

"He's worse than Cat," Adam said.

"He's not here?"

Adam shrugged and planted both feet, towering over her. "He slipped away. He's not really here, so there's not much to hang onto."

Alice nodded, looking up at him. He was trying to be intimidating, but Alice couldn't bring herself to be scared of him. Not after everything she'd done to bring him back and not now that she knew he found a way to return whenever he wanted. Thinking about it just made her tired. "What do you want?"

"Reconsidering taking me back?" he asked, a cruel grin spreading on his face.

"You can ask Peter," she told him. She turned toward the door. "I'm going back."

Adam grabbed her shoulder and spun her back around. "Then you go back," he told her. "There's no reason for you to even be here. You're not making it to the end of the semester. It doesn't matter if you pass or fail, you're going to end up as a statue, right? Might as well try to get something important done before you abandon Wonderland completely."

"That's not your choice to make, Adam." Alice turned to find Adrianna behind her, scowling at her brother. She had never seen her look angry at anyone before. "Her last days. Her choice how to spend them."

Adam shook his head and went back to the door past them. "Her friends don't even like her anymore," he said. "She might as well make herself useful."

Adrianna kept Alice from looking, taking her by the hands and keeping her facing away from the door. "He's worried about Tiger Lily, that's all," she said, smiling sympathetically. "And he's always been kind of a jerk. You didn't used to notice it when Matt was being annoying or Lance was making him shut up."

"He isn't wrong," Alice said. "I should go."

"You don't have to."

"But I should. I saw Matt. Maybe I can get him out. And I need to find someone else to put the hearts back if Tiger Lily can't."

Adrianna squeezed her hand tight when she tried to leave. She glanced at something behind Alice, but kept her voice low and leaned in when she spoke, drawing her attention. "Do you want to go?"

"I have to go."

"I mean here," she said. "Do you want to be right here right now?"

"Are you guys okay?" Sarah asked. So she was the one who caught Adrianna's attention. She came up next to her and her look softened when she saw the look on Alice's face.

Alice took a breath and made an effort to make her face neutral. Sarah only looked more concerned at the transformation, but Alice ignored it. "Fine," Alice said. "I just wanted a word with Adrianna before I headed off. I forgot. I've got a thing."

Sarah looked between the two of them before settling on Adrianna. "Does Bandersnatch mean anything to you?" she asked. When Adrianna nodded, Sarah smiled. "I knew you knew about it too."

"Do you think Alice has a chance?" Adrianna asked.

Sarah looked surprised, but it settled into a small laugh. "And you knew I was taken. Makes sense. Your brother was in there for a while with me." Her eyes grew haunted when she said it and she closed them, pushing the memory away. "No, she doesn't. It wasn't a fair bet. But I'm guessing that's not all that's been going on."

"What do you—"

"I'm not going to get into it if you don't want to," Sarah said, hands up in front of her to stop Alice. "But... If you want to at least make up with Heather before, then maybe just tell her. At least about some of this. What do you have to lose now?"

Alice nodded and said nothing. Sarah had a point. It wouldn't matter for much longer. "Maybe," she said. She let the two of them usher her back in and stayed very quiet as they started to debate what they'd be watching. The plans came together and Alice couldn't help but wonder where Adam had gotten to.

Chapter 25

Last Straw

"YOU'RE NOT THE brother I was expecting," Heather noted as Lance showed up for their movie night.

"He said you were giving him a hard time, so I'm filling in," Lance told her, though he didn't look happy about it. "Don't bother asking, he didn't tell me where he was hiding."

"Of course not," Heather muttered. She crossed her arms and regarded him carefully. "I don't—"

"I don't know where he was when he went missing, don't know who Lily is, don't know what *he* knows about Arthur the one handed boy. Does that cover everything?"

"Why do I think she knows all of that?"

Alice didn't look up, busying herself on her phone. "He knows about everything except Arthur," she said absently. Robert's game allowed her to not have to look as the conversations happened around her but still pay attention to what was happening. Heather made no effort to move away from where she was sitting, and Alice didn't want to leave just yet. Adrianna insisted that she come, that she would talk to both Heather and Adam and get them to leave her alone. Well, Heather was sort of leaving her alone.

"Ignore her," Heather said. "She keeps trying to get me to start shit with other people."

"Sounds like it's working," Lance noted. "And I really don't know where Adam went."

"He's probably hanging out with Lily somewhere," Heather said.

Alice could feel Lance's eyes on her and she shook her head. "I'm not letting him back there," she said.

Heather made a sound of irritation and stormed over to the other side of the room where the pizza was and quickly fell into loud conversation with people she liked better. At least she seemed happier over there, and she was being very good about not glaring over at Alice.

"You're not helping things," Lance said, sitting down next to her.

"I'll be in Wonderland tomorrow," she told him. She didn't look up from the game, and let it relax her. It wasn't people and it wasn't anything else that was coming for her very soon. Part of her understood why her father didn't want her to have one for so long. "And I'll stay there until I disappear. Should make everyone happy. With any luck, I'll get Matt out too."

"People are going to know you're missing."

"They're right," she said. The level she was on finished in a series of flashing lights and she looked up. It looked like they finally settled on a movie. "I'm disappearing soon. What do I have to lose anymore?"

"You don't have to—"

"You won't remember."

"Can't you at least be angry or something?"

Alice started a new level as the movie began, everyone settling into their seats. Lance fell silent, going to talk to Adrianna for a moment. Adrianna found a seat next to Alice soon after and silently urged her to put down her phone. Alice did so reluctantly, but her eyes went to the screen and she tried to get into whatever terrible movie had been chosen to be made fun of today.

As everyone else fell into making fun of the movie, Alice marveled at how easily Adrianna joined in this time. She was different now. Alice still wasn't sure what had done it. Perhaps the coma made her smarter, but it also made her less willing to believe what Alice told her and harder to convince. But it had given her the ability to catch up without needing to take a deal, and she was happier like this.

It hurt, but Adam was right. She was better off going to

Wonderland and trying to figure out as much as she could over there. It would take at least until Monday before anyone would be worried that she was gone. It might take them another week to actually expel her, or for her father to decide she wasn't supposed to be there anymore. And once that happened, maybe she had finished enough. She didn't need to be here anymore.

Even if it meant spending her last days surrounded by people telling her she was rude. Somehow, she was almost looking forward to Wonderland this time. It felt simpler.

Her phone buzzed and she looked, finding a message from Peter. That was strange. Peter had definitely been avoiding her. She glanced around to the others, all too immersed in their commentary of the movie to notice as she checked it.

Why is the crazy brother hauling the one handed asshole into the forest?

Her first question was how Peter knew about Arthur. Her second was which brother was the crazy one. The third was abruptly cut short as she put it all together.

She snapped to her feet and started to go. Adrianna grabbed her wrist, letting go as soon as Alice let out a hiss of pain. "Sorry," she said just a little too loudly, drawing eyes from around the room. She noticed, but didn't bother lowering her volume. "Where are you going?"

"Adam's about to do something stupid," Alice told her. She waved briefly to her phone and Peter's message.

"Oh, so *you* know where he is," Heather said loudly. "Why the hell is he telling you?"

"Are you talking to me again?" Alice asked bitterly. "Don't worry, I'm getting out of here."

"Where is he?"

Someone paused the movie and the room was otherwise silent. Heather was on her feet, drawing closer as Alice stood perfectly still, remaining as physically calm as she could. She had to get out of there, but Heather looked intent on getting answers before she left. And she was blocking her way out. "I'll tell him to come back."

"That's not what I asked."

"It isn't." There were too many people watching and Alice wanted nothing more than to run. She didn't want to do this here. She didn't want to do this at all. "Can I go?"

"Hell no." She seemed to get larger, widening her stance and blocking the way completely. "I tried to help you, Alice. And you ditched me for a week and *didn't tell me anything.* And you come back hurt and you don't say anything about it."

"I'm fine."

"Bullshit. Roll up your sleeves."

"It's fine."

Heather reached forward and grabbed her wrist, yanking it forward. Alice winced, but let her pull her arm forward and look at it. The bruises still decorated her arms and her wrists were still badly scratched up and scarred from the shackles.

Lance looked like he might jump in when Alice took her hand back. "It's fine," she repeated, her voice tighter. "Can you move? I'm in a bit of a hurry."

"*I don't care*," Heather told her. Alice could hear the start of a protest around her, but her attention stayed on Heather as she continued. "Why are you being such a bitch about this? Are your parents doing something shitty and making stuff hard for you? Have you just been getting kidnapped and not letting anyone know about it? Are you and Adam dating or—"

"No," Alice told her firmly. She didn't have time for this. There were too many people watching her right now and she needed to get out of there. She had to stop Adam. And, now that she was sure Heather hated her, she didn't want to be anywhere near her. "It's okay, I'm—"

"No, this is *not* okay," Heather insisted. "You have shit happening left and right and you can't just keep me in the dark and expect me to be *okay* with it! Just be honest with me and *tell me what is going on!* Why are you being so difficult?"

"*Because I'm dying, Heather!*" she yelled back at her. "I am dying. Are you happy? And now I need to make sure Adam doesn't make the same mistake. You still like *him*, right?"

Alice didn't care about the silence in the room or the eyes now on her. "Don't worry," she said. "You'll never see me again." She took a step away and she vanished in front of all of them, disappearing into the forest.

Chapter 26

Defeat

IT WASN'T UNTIL she was in the woods when she realized just what she had done. She had been keeping this from all of them for so long and now there could be no going back. After all that, she just disappeared right in front of them like it was nothing. Not to mention what she had said.

Dying.

She didn't have time to think about it. Adam was going to the Bandersnatch. She had to stop him.

The Jubjub birds were screaming. She could hear their cries even from the very edge of the dark forest. Someone was already there and walking right into them. Glancing up at the sky, she saw no sign that Peter was there, but she didn't know if she could have spotted him. The moon was partially covered by clouds and she could barely see the ground further into the forest.

Alice got exactly as close to the Jubjubs as she could, outside the ring of fog that hid the Bandersnatch's lair. Either they were very happy or very upset and she didn't know which. It didn't matter, their cries echoing in her head and drawing out every horrifying image and dark thought that she could imagine. Hearts without bodies beat heavy in her ears and visions of Neverland floated across her eyes.

With a deep breath, she made one last step and was in the lair of the Bandersnatch. She tried not to think about how easy it was this time and wiped the tears from her eyes as she looked around. Inside, it was not brighter but everything shone. The moon was full in the sky here to illuminate the glittering dark stone. At least the garden didn't look any bigger.

Most importantly, Adam was not here.

"You are playing a dangerous game, child."

The Bandersnatch rose from the floor, his body large and towering over her. All four white eyes cracked open and narrowed on her. Alice could feel the discontent coming off of him, saw that he didn't quite form into a shape and blended into the dark sky above him.

Alice took another deep breath, trying to steady herself. "A friend of mine is coming to make a deal. I'm asking you not to let him do it."

Those white eyes came closer and Alice was surrounded by darkness. "And what power do you think you have, child?"

he asked, demanding an answer she couldn't give. "What makes you think I would permit you to interfere with any of my deals?"

Alice stayed very quiet, eyes wide as she stared back up at him. Her heart was pounding so loudly that she thought it might deafen her. The feeling drained out of her extremities and she couldn't feel her knees as they dropped to the ground. "Please," she said at last. "He doesn't know. He doesn't *understand.*"

"None of them did," he said, indicating the garden. "Just as you did not, child. But a deal is a deal. And if he comes, he will be permitted to ask anything, provided he pays the appropriate price." The Bandersnatch turned back on her suddenly, engulfing her vision once more. "Regret is a normal part of life, child. I provide precisely the services requested, nothing more or less. And you will not be permitted to interfere."

"Can I at least talk to him first?" Her words were soft and desperate. "He doesn't know."

"You could have told him before," the Bandersnatch told her. "Or you could have won our bet and made it impossible for him. Unless you have an attempt to make now, Alice Liddell."

Alice backed away. This had been stupid. Reckless. She knew she had to stop Adam from making a mistake, from giving someone else to the Bandersnatch, but she should have stopped *him.* The Bandersnatch was not one to listen to her, not knowing that he was going to have her soon enough. Although now, looking at those eyes, she thought she saw a hunger there that was ready to take his reward early.

"I will not harm you," the Bandersnatch told her. "Perhaps Wonderland's hero would like to watch. His desire may interest you."

Alice opened her mouth, not sure if it was to protest or defend herself, but no words came out. She very suddenly couldn't move, couldn't speak, could barely even breathe. She was trapped, locked away inside of something and very suddenly in a different place than she had been. The dark glass around her didn't conceal the throne next to her, or the young man who stumbled across the threshold into the Bandersnatch's lair.

Even from here, she could see Adam trembling as he collapsed to the ground. He pushed himself gently up, his eyes wide as he took in the vast space around him, the darkness that surrounded him and the silver of the statues that made up the garden. He breathed a curse and got to his feet, drinking in the world he'd walked into.

"Hello Adam Case," the Bandersnatch said from his throne. "Have you come to make me an offer?"

"What do I get for getting rid of those birds?" he asked bitterly.

There was amusement as the Bandersnatch waited for him

to approach. "I grew so tired of people stumbling onto me without intent," he said. "She placed them there so that she could get your brother back. Perhaps if you return Evan Case to my garden, I will allow you to remove them once more."

Adam hesitated only a moment before he reached behind him. He glanced back at the garden of statues. Of people whose faces he couldn't recall, and grabbed the boy he brought with him. Arthur was slowly coming around behind him and Adam dragged him across the stone floor to the Bandersnatch. "I'm here to make a different deal. I think you know this guy."

He dropped Arthur at his side and he groaned as his head hit the ground. He curled, eyes bleary as he looked up to the Bandersnatch.

The Bandersnatch was more curious now. Alice could swear she heard chuckle escape him. "Arthur Pendragon," he said. "You make a very enticing offer. Not often someone brings me a king to trade. Unfortunate that he appears to be broken."

"I hear you'll take anyone to make a deal," Adam said. "Bigger the deal, the more valuable the person I'm handing over, right? And this is the guy who trapped you the last time, so I'm thinking it should be enough for me to ask anything."

"And you are ready to sacrifice him for your wishes," the Bandersnatch said.

"First he assaults my sister, then he starts stalking her," Adam said bitterly. "I think I'm fine with it."

"She is the fairest— *Ugh!*"

Adam gave him a kick to shut him up. Alice stared from inside her prison, looking down at Arthur. Had he been doing that? Adrianna hadn't mentioned it, but Adrianna was so much different now. Maybe she had learned to keep secrets on top of everything else. Alice knew that he had appeared to watch her, but now that she thought on in more, she realized Adrianna had always been there. And looking at him now, Arthur was making no excuses.

Adam let out an irritated groan. "So you'll take him?"

"Tell me your desire."

"I desire you trap yourself in that damn book again," Arthur choked out.

Adam turned to kick him once more, but the Bandersnatch descended upon Arthur, a large black creature with four eyes picking him up by the chest and looking him over. "Your lands are gone. Your wizard trapped himself in that form and drove him mad. You don't even have all of your years or limbs any longer. You have fallen so far and, for all the suffering you have caused me, you are now mine. It will be a pleasure to have you in my garden."

"Our deal?" Adam insisted, growing annoyed.

"Tell me, Adam Case," he said, casting a line of black over Arthur's mouth and silencing whatever he was about to say. "What do you desire?"

"Wonderland."

That gained the attention of the four eyes. "You wish all of it?"

Adam shook his head. "Alice won't save it and she won't let me go back so I can save it, so I want you to do it. Put all the hearts back, take the books out, get rid of the Queen of Hearts."

Alice could hear the slick smile in his voice. "And you do not want to try and pardon Alice Liddell from our little bet?"

"She wouldn't save Wonderland even if she wasn't going into that garden of yours," he said. He glanced back at the statues. When he looked back, Alice could see the discomfort in his eyes, though he kept his shoulders square and jaw set. "Take her for all I care. Just save Wonderland."

Alice went cold and immediately chided herself for it. She knew Adam didn't care about her. Of course he would let her go. Her stomach remained clenched tight, but she knew it was only because he actually said it. She wasn't surprised that he felt that way.

The Bandersnatch waited for a moment, a low hum echoing out of him before he spoke again. "I had expected more of a reaction out of you," he said. "But no matter. It cannot be done with Arthur Pendragon alone."

The dark glass went clear and she saw Adam's face drop. He stared at her and his jaw opened to speak. Quickly he shut it again, thinking better of it and looking back at her defiantly. There would be no apology and he did not feel bad that he said it. There were more pressing matters. "What do you mean it can't be done?" he asked.

"You want Wonderland saved," the Bandersnatch told him. "Another world entirely. One that he doesn't give me access to. I will need someone from Wonderland to point my way." A cruel lilt appeared in his voice. "If you are patient, you can return when Alice has properly failed to accomplish our bet. If you can remember her enough to know she is gone. It is unlikely that you will."

Adam's eyes went wide and his breath caught in his throat. His eyes flickered back to the barrier, haunted as his hands started to twitch. For as brave as he was being now, for all the recklessness, he didn't want to come back. She didn't know if it was the Bandersnatch or the haunting cries of the Jubjub birds, but it was clear that he wanted this to be settled here and now.

"I could give her to you now," Adam said. "I can make a deal with her instead."

There was something dangerous in how sharp his eyes became. "Are you trying to offer me spoils that I have already won, child?"

"What about me?" he offered quickly. "I was there for a long time. You can take me."

Alice tried to scream, to tell him not to do it. She didn't think he would be that much of an idiot to give himself up, but she could do nothing but watch. After how hard she'd tried to get him back, Adam was going to disappear, and willingly. But he didn't have to. Alice was already doing that, and Wonderland would be fine.

The Bandersnatch drew closer, dropping Arthur to the ground as he regarded Adam more closely. There was approval in the way his eyes moved and in how his body shifted and curled around him. "You would give up yourself? It has been a very long time since I have seen such self-sacrifice."

"Will it work?"

"Yes."

"Then do it."

No. Alice wouldn't let him do it. She watched as the Bandersnatch closed in around him, looking around for anything she could do. She could see the moon reflected in the ground, could see Arthur push himself away from his reflection. Could see herself in the ground staring back up at her.

And then she could see none of it. Beneath them, stretching until the edges of the Bandersnatch's lair, was the sky looking back. It was tinged pink and there was a single cloud in the sky, one that carried a castle for birds. It was a bright day and the sun shone up from the formerly black expanse. Foliage peaked in around the side, and Alice knew she was looking up from the lake of soda in Wonderland.

Alice strained in her prison, concentrating hard to keep her thoughts from wavering. She could not close her eyes or block out anything that might distract her. She could see the surprise on Arthur's face as he scrambled and tried to save himself from the emptiness below him, watched as the statues in the garden fell away into it, and did nothing to stop them.

The Bandersnatch fell through, the dark shape slipping under the floor and vanishing from sight, though a few final words echoed through the air. "Well played, child." There was no malice, no anger as he fell away. His kingdom cracked and crumbled in a deafening roar as it went crashing down into the vast expanse.

Nothing held her up anymore. The moon was gone now and she was surrounded by darkness. Or maybe she had shut her eyes. She fell limp and collapsed, letting the weariness overtake her.

CHAPTER 27

Consequences of Victory

SUNLIGHT BEAT DOWN on her face. Alice was sore lying on the hard, flat ground. She didn't know how long she had been there, or where she was, but she found it hard to be bothered by it. Wherever she was, she felt like she was at home. Her arm was numb underneath her and she wasn't comfortable to be sure, but she didn't open her eyes yet.

She didn't want to move. She didn't need to move right now.

What happened came back to her slowly. The revelation that Arthur had been following Adrianna. Adam trying to trade him. Adam offering himself. Alice turning the whole of the Bandersnatch's lair into a mirror and dropping him into Wonderland.

The Bandersnatch. Gone. She was going to live.

The thought didn't leave her as happy as she thought it

would. Numbness settled in where the celebration should have been. That wasn't all that happened, after all. She had yelled at Heather. She had told everyone she was dying. She promised she would never return and she had disappeared in front of all of them.

And now she had to go back.

Slowly, she cracked open her eyes and saw black stone all around her. Her heart sank, seeing the dark throne in front of her. Everything was shining black stone, just as it had been before she dropped it into Wonderland. If it had dropped into Wonderland at all. The Bandersnatch was still there.

"Awake, child." The Bandersnatch peeled off of the ground and those four eyes watched over her. He was a large cat, watching over her and waiting for her to get up.

Alice pushed herself up and sighed. "It didn't work," she said.

"On the contrary," he said. He was pleased, Alice noting how his tail swished behind him. "For once, one of you heroes has won a bet."

"But…" Alice looked around, seeing that this was exactly the same lair as before. But this place still felt different. It felt just a little more mad. "Are we in Wonderland?"

"We are. You have won our bet."

"I won," she said, looking around again. "Where's Adam?"

The Bandersnatch let out something that might have been

a laugh. "Neither Adam Case or Arthur Pendragon fell. They remain in your world. Although, if you did decide to offer me Arthur Pendragon, I could be convinced to resolve any problems you may be having in this world."

Alice ignored him. After all of this, she wasn't about to go sacrificing people now. What else needed to be settled here? She looked up and back to the garden. "You need to put them all back, then."

"I shall. It is another world they must return to, so it will take me some time." A smile was in his voice as he spoke. "You are not pleased by your victory."

"I still have to go back." Back to Heather after she yelled at her. Back to her friends, who had now seen what she could do. Back to school where she had only barely paid attention all year. Back to her parents whose divorce she was now going to have to deal with.

Alice let out a breath. If she was already in Wonderland, she could try to get a few things done. Tell Tiger Lily that she was going to continue coming back. Put back some hearts. Maybe help figure out what they could do with the Queen of Hearts. Right now, Wonderland was much less complicated than Lucena Academy and she was not eager to leave. "How long you think I can stay here before I have to go back?" she asked.

"You have entertained me, child," the Bandersnatch said.

"Your absence will not be noticed until I return the last of my garden to your world."

"Okay," Alice said. "Thank you." She was so tired. Emotionally and physically, she had completely exhausted herself and she couldn't keep herself in check any longer. One thought refused to stay down and echoed through her mind as she made her way to the White Rabbit's house.

It would have been nice if it was over.

CHAPTER 28

Graduation

SOMETHING WAS DIFFERENT ever since that movie night, Adrianna could feel it. It wasn't just the blow out between Alice and Heather, or the fact that Alice was now actively avoiding hanging out with them. That she could understand, as unhappy as it made her that they couldn't work it out. It was something more than that.

Sarah insisted for about a week that Alice wasn't even there anymore, but that wasn't true. Of course Alice had been there. Where else would she have been? Even Adam, who had decided very suddenly that Alice was not worth the effort of even thinking about, said she was still around. But soon Sarah had let that rest and her focus was on person after person who sought her out, people Adrianna didn't think she had ever even talked to before now wanting a word with her. After a time, Adrianna noticed every single one of those people avoided Adam like a plague, casting a look his way that Adrianna didn't want to speculate on.

The strangeness came to a head the night before graduation. Finals had finally worn down and the dorms had been mostly celebratory. They were all just happy to be done with it all and chattering in the common area. There was a whisper that someone had brought alcohol, but no one knew who or where it was. It didn't matter; they had enough to enjoy themselves for now and Adrianna didn't want this to be broken up by the dorm advisors.

The mood was broken instead with a single action. Wyatt walking up to Nike and, with barely a word of warning, he slugged him hard in the face. Wyatt, who Adrianna had never known to be anything but kind and gentle and sweet, didn't stop at that, jumping on him when Nike tried to fight back, insisting that Nike knew just what he had done.

Adam had been next to Adrianna when it happened and he jumped in soon after, grabbing Wyatt around the arms and pulling him off. When he tried to break free of Adam's grip, Adam pulled him aside into the deserted halls leading to the study rooms. Trailing immediately after them, Sarah looked worried.

Adrianna didn't know what was happening and followed as well. It didn't make any sense. Wyatt and Nike lived together, had gone this whole day without so much of an inkling that anything might be amiss. Thinking back, Adrianna tried to think of anything that might have happened, but she didn't know either of them well enough anymore to pick anything out. The party atmosphere was so suddenly uncomfortable, and she followed to see what Sarah was so interested in.

Wyatt had already pulled himself out of Adam's arms when she got there, but Adam kept him from going any further. "*It was worth it,*" Wyatt told them. "He took years from me. *Years.*"

"Me too," Sarah told him. "But no one knows what happened, Wyatt. No one even knows you were gone."

"I've been told." There was a venom in the words, one that Adrianna never thought she would hear out of Wyatt. She had really liked him once, but she couldn't see that boy in him anymore. "I hate this."

"You'll get it," Sarah assured him. "It's going to take a couple days."

"I can't believe you're hanging out with *him* now," Wyatt told her. His eyes cut back to Adam, that familiar look of malice in them that she had seen from the others. "Do you know what he did?"

"I didn't *do* anything," Adam said. "I don't know what all of you think—"

"You think no one knows?" Wyatt asked. "We were watching. We aren't going to forget."

"Wyatt," Sarah said loudly enough to draw his attention. "How many left?"

"I was the last one," he said. "You're waiting for Alice?"

Sarah nodded.

"You'll see her tomorrow, I think." He looked back at Adam, the scowl returning to his face. "I'm getting out of here. See you around Sarah. Adrianna."

Adrianna didn't stop him as he stormed past and watched him go. Sarah looked relieved, at least. Adam, on the other hand, looked like he had seen a ghost. He shook the look off his face quickly enough, but Adrianna had to wonder just how much she had missed. There were a lot of people not telling her something. The next time she saw Alice, she would have to ask what was going on.

"SARAH THINKS YOU'RE missing," Adrianna told Alice the next morning as they got ready for graduation. She had been there in the morning as she always was, a bit of a slope to her shoulders as she got ready. She tied her long blond hair back and assembled her makeup for the ceremony. "Are your parents going to be here today?"

"No," Alice said, though she didn't sound sad about it. "Dad's busy. Mom's on the other side of the country. Lori couldn't get the time off of work. Middle school isn't really an important one."

"It was still hard!" Adrianna said. She didn't know how she made it through school this long. Since waking up from her coma, everything had been a lot easier. Somehow, her mind was clear and she could actually put together what she was being taught. It was probably the easiest round of tests she had ever taken, but she couldn't forget how hard it was to get there.

Alice stayed quiet at first before putting on that quizzical expression. "You want me to do your makeup?"

"Sure!" Adrianna went across the room to sit on Alice's bed, letting her make her up. She looked at her phone, changing the music lightly drifting through the room to fill the quiet. Adrianna was figuring out how to do her own makeup slowly, but Alice was still better at it than she was.

Her phone buzzed in her hands and Adrianna looked down to see a message from Sarah, who was better at makeup than all of them. She had an advantage since her mom had made her fortune creating makeup and she had grown up around more types than Adrianna could ever imagine.

"Sarah's coming," Adrianna told her.

"I'm done," Alice told her, putting away the last brush and

handing Adrianna the lip gloss to put on herself. When the knock came at the door, Alice went to get it.

Sarah threw her arms around Alice as soon as she saw her. She didn't hear whatever it was Sarah muttered in her ear, only seeing Alice's confusion turn uncomfortable and almost bashful as she let the hug continue to happen. Sarah squeezed her tight for a little longer before letting her go and letting herself in.

"And you look good," Sarah added, smiling. She ushered Alice out of the doorway before she shut it behind her. "But that's not why I'm here. You need to tell me what happened. Did he really just let you go? What have you been doing the last month? I was worried and thought I was going *nuts* because no one would admit you weren't here."

Alice shrugged, shrinking away from her and wandering back to her bed. "I had to finish a couple things," Alice said. "It took longer than I thought."

"You weren't here?" Adrianna asked, confused. But she remembered seeing her here. She remembered waking up and seeing Alice, remembered seeing her in the evenings and at nights. "But where else would she be?"

"Wonderland," Sarah said. "That's what it's called, right?"

Alice stayed quiet and sank down onto her bed. "The Bandersnatch is gone now," she said. "No one else can make any more deals with him. It'll never happen again."

"Because you won."

"Yeah."

Adrianna watched as Sarah looked pleased by that fact and Alice tried very hard to smile about her victory. There was something there that didn't feel authentic. It was more like the whole thing was making her tired, like she wanted to forget about it and move on.

Adrianna could understand. This year had been hard on all of them. Adrianna had been in a coma for part of it, but it had been a difficult year of trying to not fall to the Bandersnatch. Now that Alice was free of its clutches, she was able to go and finish up her work in Wonderland and maybe even enjoy it. For all she complained, Adrianna had a hard time really understanding what was so terrible about the place. She had only been once, but even now she could barely remember if anyone had really gotten hurt.

There was something about it, though. She knew there was something terrible about it itching at the back of her mind, but she couldn't quite remember what...

"Well, I'm going to get going," Sarah said, smiling and letting herself out. "I'll see you guys down there."

Adrianna smiled and watched her go. She had so many questions, but she could wait until after to ask Alice what she was talking about. She knew Alice had been here. And if she hadn't been, Alice would tell her soon enough.

She took Alice's hand and gave her a squeeze. She smiled back at her and waited for Alice to get up. "Come on," she said. "We did it. We don't want to be late, right?"

About the Author

TANYA LISLE IS a novelist from Metro Vancouver, British Columbia, who has series littered across genres from supernatural horror to young adult fantasy. She began writing in elementary school, when she started turning homework assignments into short stories and continued this trend well into university. While attending Simon Fraser University, she developed an appreciation for public domain crossovers and cross-platform narratives. She has a shelf full of notebooks with more story ideas than pens lost to the depths of her bag. Now she writes incessantly in hopes of finishing all of them.

Thankfully, her cat, Remy, has figured out how to shut off Tanya's computer when she needs to take a break.